T0193455

AT THE
RIGHT PLACE
AT THE
RIGHT TIME

LES SONKSEN

Order this book online at www.trafford.com
or email orders@trafford.com

Most Trafford titles are also available at major online book retailers.

Print information available on the last page.

ISBN: 978-1-6987-1591-9 (sc)
ISBN: 978-1-6987-1592-6 (e)

Library of Congress Control Number: 2023922821

Trafford rev. 12/26/2023

 www.trafford.com

North America & international
toll-free: 844-688-6899 (USA & Canada)
fax: 812 355 4082

ACKNOWLEDGEMENT

The valuable help of Detective Michael Williams of his police department is greatly appreciated. As a beta reader, he provided the correct terminology in detective work plus methods used to solve crimes.

Another critical help was that of Avery Gregurich as a beta reader. He is an editor and contributor for the OUR IOWA magazine. He corrected punctuation and some spelling I missed plus what the computer reader didn't find.

The staff members of Trafford Publishing gave important assistance in the steps and procedures to accomplish the printed version.

CHAPTER 1
TOBIAS RODRIQUEZ

My birth certificate states that I'm Tobias Rodriquez. However, everybody calls me Toby. I enjoy hanging around with my pals in the great city of Aurora, Colorado.

On reflection, have you been at the right place at the right time, or perhaps, at the wrong place at the wrong time? Or other combinations? Somehow, for some time now in my life, these situations have taken place. Why? I've been wrestling with that situation many times. Here goes!

Minding my own business on a bright sunny Friday morning, I was moseying on my motor bike. I was going north on Sable Road to buy school supplies for my senior year in high school starting next week. The light turned red at E. Florida Avenue. As I stopped, a car on my left was burning rubber when the light turned green. He sped across the intersection, veered left, tires screeching as he braked in front of an office building midway down the block. He jumped out and ran up the sidewalk to meet a lady who had just left the building.

I thought, *Really has a fling to see sweetheart.*

I was badly mistaken. He grabbed her around the waist, half lifting her as she tried walking tippy toe. I could hear her yelling but too far away to understand what she was saying.

He held her with his left arm, opened the back door and literally threw her in the back seat. He slammed the door shut, jumped behind the wheel and shot down the street.

I could hardly wait for the light to turn green so I could move closer to read the plate number. Speeding over the limit, I seemed to be getting closer but the light turned red on Exposition Avenue and I had to stop. I thought about running the red light, but the traffic was too heavy. I had a difficult time keeping my eyes on the blue car because more cars were building up behind it and I lost sight. *Darn stoplights anyway! Never catch car now.*

CHAPTER 2
DIXIE TALLMAN AND EX-HUSBAND, DAN AUSTIN

"**S**low down, Dan! You're going to get us in a wreck!" I shouted.

"Shut up, I know what I'm doing!" retorted Dan. I continued racing down Sable Road, braking quickly, while pulling into a parking spot. He ignored the signed stating PARKING PROHIBITED. He turned to look back at Dixie. "I'm sorry I manhandled you and threw you in the car. I was angry because I knew you were getting my cash from your account."

"Just a darn minute my ex-husband. You agreed to the $90,000 as part of our divorce settlement. Quit your bitching! You're drunk! Or high on cocaine!"

"Okay! Whatever! With all that money on you, do you have your revolver ready to use should you need to?"

"Yes, I do. Why the questioning?"

"May I see it and check it for your safety?"

I opened my purse and gave him my revolver.

"Hum-m. Yes, you learned good. You have a full magazine of shells. You have a bullet in the chamber ready to shoot. The safety is on. Good girl!"

"You taught me how to do all that. I haven't forgotten. Are you taking me for a dummy?"

He placed the gun to his temple. "I hope you rot in prison trying to spend my money." With that, he pulled the trigger. His head slumped forward resting on the steering wheel. The right-hand landing in the passenger seat with the gun falling from his hand.

For several seconds, I was in a state of shock with the loud crack of the gun. Then, reality hit me. "WHY YOU SON-OF-A-BITCH! YOU SHOOT YOURSELF WITH MY GUN AND MADE IT LOOK LIKE I MURDERED YOU! DAMN FOOL! I ONCE LOVED YOU, NOW I'LL ALWAYS HATE YOUR GUTS," I shouted out loud. *Need to get out of here. Can't be caught sitting here with dead man.*

I grabbed the gun from the front seat and crammed it in my purse. Using a knuckle, I pushed the door latch and kicked the door open. Snatching my valise, I bolted out the door and started running down the sidewalk. I saw a city bus stopping at the corner and a lady getting off. I yelled out, "TELL THE DRIVER TO HOLD THE BUS FOR ME!"

As I climbed the steps, breathlessly, I managed to say, "Thank you for waiting. How much is the fare?"

"Depends how far you're going, Ma'am. A dollar fifty takes you to the end of the line. If getting off sooner, I can give you a transfer ticket."

I tried to open my purse with one hand. The bus lurched forward and I had to quickly grab a bar to keep from falling.

"Take a seat, Ma'am, before you fall. Pay when you get off."

Riding down the street, my thoughts were bouncing every which way. *How could he shoot himself? Damn fool! Made it appear I did it. Still love him. Seven years great marriage. Booze and drugs changed him. Mean as hell! Restraining orders useless. Need other clothes. Get rid of gun. Can't have cops find it on me. Divorce now. Alone. What do I do?*

CHAPTER 3
TOBY

I could hardly wait for the darn light to turn green. *Can I find blue car in all this slow-moving traffic? Might as well forget about it. Just get my school stuff.* But as I toddled down the street, I saw the same car parked in a No Parking zone. When I pulled up beside the driver's window, the man was leaning over the steering wheel. A hole on his left side of his face was oozing blood. *Did she shoot him? Back passenger door open?* I shot a glance in all directions, but did not see the lady that was wearing a white skirt and a yellow blouse and holding tight to a small black bag when I was watching her being abducted.

Pulling out my cellphone, I speed dialed my brother-in-law, Michael Dorsey, a detective with the Aurora Police Department. No answer. I punched in 911. I told the dispatcher the discovery and location.

"Stay with the car. I'll get squad cars in the area to rush to the place," she said. While waiting, I noticed a bus going down the street some distance away. *Could have boarded bus in that short of time?*

I only waited around two minutes when two squad cars came speeding down Sable Road with one car pulling up behind the blue car, and the other parking beside it with lights flashing.

Again, I related to the officers what I had witnessed. The one sergeant was scribbling the details on a pad as I spoke. He asked me to repeat some details. "Since I didn't see the lady, I did see a bus in the distance. She might have been able to board it."

The second sergeant grabbed his shoulder mic. "Any cars in the vicinity of Sable Avenue stop any bus and apprehend a woman wearing a yellow blouse and a white skirt."

The police department's forensic team parked behind the police car on the street, its lights flashing. I watched the team taking several pictures. Two were dusting the interior for finger prints. I noticed a team member remove a plastic glove from the victim's right hand. *That's very strange,* I thought. The drivers of the forensic team and the squad car backed up and blocked the street. I watched them searching the pavement. *What in the world are they looking for?* I thought. After some time, the drivers repositioned the cars for the traffic to start moving again. Then I heard one policeman say, "It's impossible to find a .22 slug on the pavement. It may have gone further than this street."

The coroner parked behind the police car. I watched as he made a brief examination. I heard him say, "It appears that death was caused by a small bullet, perhaps a .22 caliber. Our lab can pinpoint the death precisely." The coroner signed some papers and gave them to one sergeant.

The speaker on the sergeant's phone blurted out. "We were able to stop two buses, but the lady was not on either. One driver recalled a lady with a white skirt and yellow blouse had gotten off at the last stop which was E. Centrepoint Drive. We drove to the intersection, asked the business and people on the street, but no one had seen the lady in question."

CHAPTER 4
DIXIE TALLMAN

The bus stopped. *Need to get off. Clothes like flag! Need change.* As I got off the bus, I asked, "Did I see a Walmart store on our way?"

"Yes. I could have stopped there if you had made it known to me. There will be a bus on the other side of Sable going south. Tell the driver to stop near it for you."

"Thanks. I'm in a hurry so I'll catch a taxi."

By luck, a taxi stopped near me. He helped the passenger get out. I hailed the driver and he waited for me. "Please take me to Walmart." The driver opened the door for me and I got in.

Again, thoughts fill my mind. *Asked to see gun. Commented my being ready to use it. Then said, Have a great time spending my money while rotting in prison." Put revolver to temple and pulled trigger. How could he do such a thing? Panicked! Had to get away. Remembered retrieving gun from front seat. Kicked door open. Grabbed money. Bolted out of door. Running down sidewalk. Yelling at lady to have driver wait. Why? Why did he do this to me?* I wiped the tears rolling down my cheeks with a finger.

The taxi stopped at the store entrance. The driver opened the door for me. I slid out while opening my purse. "How much do I owe you?"

"The fare is six dollars."

"Here's ten. Thanks for the quick trip."

He pocketed the money. "We aim to please our customers."

7

I entered the store and hesitated while looking for the ladies' section. Spying it, I negotiated the crowded aisles. There was a large selection of skirts and blouses to examine. My eyes were drawn to a rack of pants suits in various shades of colors. I like this Slimtacular khaki-colored pants with a brown rayon blouse, and a quilted mélange vest for cooler weather.

A clerk approached me. "May I help you?"

"Yes. Can I try these on? Do you have a dressing room?"

"We certainly do. Follow me."

I removed my blouse and skirt and slipped into the new items. *Should help blend with crowd.* Leaving the dressing room, I approached the clerk. "These are so just right that I'll wear them. Can you place my old clothes in a bag?"

"Yes, I can." She took the clothes from me and headed to the check out counter. She rang up the purchase. "That will be $79. 85."

I opened my purse. "Is cash okay with you?"

"Certainly."

I gave the clerk a hundred-dollar bill. She placed the $20.15 change in my hand. "Thanks for shopping at Walmart. I'll cut off the price tags and designer's info cards. The colors suit you very well."

"Thank you for the compliment." Placing my purse strap on my shoulder, I picked up my valise and left the store. I saw a waste container and shoved my old clothes in it. *Good riddance! Now what to do. Get back to car. Taxi again? The bus?* I saw a lady headed for her car.

"Excuse me. Would you be heading south on Sable?"

The lady surveyed me from head to toe carefully. "Why do you ask?"

"I'll pay you twenty dollars. I need to go to the corner of East Florida. The last taxi driver started talking sexy stuff. I don't know when the bus will be coming."

The lady moved toward her car. "Be pleased to help you, but you don't need to pay me."

"That is so kind of you." I took off my jacket for I figured the car would be hot. We got in the car.

"I'm Ann." She immediately rolled down all the windows. "Cars get so hot parked in the sun." At Florida Street, Ann stopped and I got out. "Thanks. Really appreciate the lift."

Ann smiled. "You are welcome. Have a good day!"

Good day? Hardly. I spotted my car where I had left it. As I approached it, I saw a ticket under the wiper blade. *Oh, no, now what do I do? Pay or ignore it!"* I shoved it in my purse and got into my car. I immediately rolled down all the windows. I sat behind the wheel with my hands resting at the top. *Now what to do? Police probably found Dan. DMV identified him. Thank goodness changed to maiden name. Do police know who I am? Not yet, I hope. Go to apartment. Pack suitcases. Where can I go?*

I pulled out my cellphone and googled for map of Wyoming and then Montana. I studied the possible places. *Montana might be place to go. Fly to Hawaii. Get lost.* I looked at my case containing the money. *Should last a while. Credit cards leave trails. Airline tickets leave trails. Darn!*

I studied the places in Montana, finding the small towns of Frombery, Bridger, Silesia, Boyd and Edgar. *Drive through each. Find one that's possible. Start business. Use crafting skills. Hobby income. No social security. No tax schedules.*

I drove to my apartment. Throwing part of my clothes, some bathroom and grooming items, and two pair of shoes into two suitcases, I realized much had to be left behind. I went to the kitchen and pulled two bottles of water and a carton of donuts from the refrigerator, placing them in a paper bag. Grabbing a pen and piece of paper, I wrote a note to my landlord.

Dear Helen. I had to leave in a hurry and no time to clean the place. My deposit can pay for any expenses. Keep anything you like and throw the rest away. Rents paid up. Thank you for your friendship. I don't know when I'll be back.

Dixie.

I dumped my suitcases in the back seat. Throwing the bag of food and the water in the front seat, I backed out the drive way and headed for I-25. *Need to get the hell out of Dodge before cops find me.*

CHAPTER 5
DETECTIVE MICHAEL DORSEY

I usually do not work on Saturdays unless it's an emergency. My supervisor called to tell me a file was on my desk and it was urgent. I walked into my office and found all the material of Dan Austin's' death. My supervisor wants me to handle the case. I started pouring over the police reports, the forensic findings, the coroner's statements, the DMV documents, and the list of items found in the car, and in the man's billfold. *Toby certainly had detailed report what he saw. Really proud of him. Very observant.*

I read through all the paper work again. *Must have missed something. Nope. Nothing more. Need to get off my duff. See places. Talk to people. Somebody knows something. Need to find those people.*

I drove to the place where Austin was shot, studying the complete area, pacing the distance from where the car was to the place where the bus had stopped. *Possible time to catch bus. Got off the bus E, Centre Point. Ask for taxi? Probably.*

I drove to the intersection where she exited the bus, asking the business people if any had seen a woman wearing the white skirt and yellow blouse yesterday. No one saw anything. When I got back to my car, I saw two checker-colored taxis. Pulling out my cellphone, I touched the numbers I saw on the cabs.

"Hello. Checkered Taxi Company. May I help you?"

"Yes. This is Detective Michael Dorsey with the APD. Do you have a record of a fare from the intersection of Sable Road and E. Centre Point Drive on Friday around 11 a.m.?"

"Let me check our records. Yes, Detective Dorsey, we had a lady hail a cab that had just discharged another fare. She requested to go to Walmart."

"Thank you for the information."

"You're welcome."

I drove to Walmart, parked, and entered the store. *What did she buy? Food? Maybe. House hold items? Possibly. Clothes? More likely.* Seeing a clerk, "I'm Detective Michael Dorsey. Can you direct me to the loss prevention office to review your security videos. I need to find out about a person of interest in a case study."

"Yes, I'll take you there. Helen, this is Detective Dorsey who needs to see our security tapes about a person of interest in his case study."

"Thank you, Ann. Yes, Detective Dorsey, how may I help you?"

"Would it be possible to view your video from last Friday at around 11 a.m. or later? I have information that she came into the store about that time. I'm trying to find the lady relative to the death of her ex-husband."

"Yes, I can help you, Detective. Let me back up our system to last Friday at 10:45 and advance forward."

I watched closely. "She is wearing a yellow blouse and a white skirt." The recording was very sharp as I watched the people coming into the store. "There she is! Can we follow her as to where she went in the store?"

"Yes, I need to switch to different camera recordings." We watched as she moved to the women's clothing area.

"Thank you, Helen. You have helped me considerably."

I found my way to the ladies' section. Looking for a clerk, I saw one arranging skirts. "Do you remember seeing a lady in a white shirt and yellow blouse buying any clothes yesterday?"

"Sorry, I don't. Perhaps June did. She's on break," looking at her watch. "She should be back shortly."

"Thank you. I'll wait for, ah, ah, June."

I didn't have to wait long before a clerk approached. "Are you, June?"

"Yes, I am. How may I help you?"

"I'm Detective Michael Dorsey with the APD. Did you wait on a lady, per chance, wearing a white skirt and yellow blouse yesterday?"

"Yes, I do remember. A very beautiful person." She moved to a display of pants. "She bought a pair of khaki pants, brown blouse and this attractive jacket. She went into the changing room to check the fitting, then wore them when leaving."

"Now we're getting somewhere! Did she pay by credit card or cash?"

"She paid with cash. We don't ask for any names on this type of transaction."

"Oh, darn. What did she do with the clothes she was wearing?"

"I placed them in a plastic bag which she took with her."

Taking out my cellphone, "May I get a picture of what she purchased for ID purposes?"

"Yes, but is she in some kind of trouble?"

"We don't know yet. Just following leads of a case."

June pulled a pair of pants and the jacket from the display. "I'll hold them against me."

"Great!" I snapped a picture, then checked the results. "This may help. Thanks."

I found my way back to the entrance and started for my car, scanning the area. *Can't believe it. Tillie the Street Lady. Haven't seen her couple years.* I walked to where she was sitting on a cement step with her shopping cart beside her with her worldly possessions filling the basket. "Tillie, how are you? Haven't seen you since I was on the street beat."

"Sergeant Mike! Dats you? Can't see you for sportin' that hair on yer face."

"It's Detective Mike, now, Tillie."

"Oh, theys boot you up, Ha?"

"Something like that. Tillie, have you seen a lady that was here yesterday wearing a yellow blouse and a white skirt?"

"Sure enough did. She goes in with does colors and come out brown colors."

"What did she do? Where did she go?"

"She gets in car with lady. But first she puts bag in trash barrel. I goes get it." Tillie stood up and pulled a plastic sack from the cart and gave it to Mike.

I opened the sack. "These are her clothes! Have you pulled them out and handled them, Tillie?"

"No, sir. Only looks in sack. Puts em in my wardrobe."

I pulled out my billfold. "Tillie, can I buy them for $20?"

"Oh, yes, Mike. Youse is good like. Sure miss you. Your wife will like em."

"How is life treating you, Tillie?"

"Good. Folks helps me lots. Food. Money. Clothes. People pay me to hold rope to hold doggies while shoppin. Cars too hot for doggies. I stay here. Life good like."

"Tillie, I need to go. Be good to yourself. You helped to find the lady who wore these." He looked in the sack once more. *Important evidence.*

CHAPTER 6

DIXIE

Getting hungry. Cheyenne ahead. I entered the city and saw advertising for The Albany. *That's the place.* I pulled out my cellphone and googled the directions. Following the streets, I was soon sitting in a booth and ordering dinner.

Food hit spot. Stay here at hotel? Two hours to Douglas. Get motel there.

As I was deciding what to do, I placed my hands on the edge of the back seat cushion. My fingers were in a space. I looked down and saw a small space between the back of the cushion and the back of the wooden seat. I kicked my foot back. There was solid board. *A box seat! Place to hide revolver.*

I slipped the gun from my purse under the table. Using my napkin, I dipped it in my water glass, then wiped off any finger prints. I slipped the revolver into the crack and heard the thud when it hit the floor. I looked around, but no one seem to have heard the sound. *Sometime before found, I hope. Good riddance!*

I paid for the meal, went to my car and found my way back to I-25. *Douglas, here I come!*

I entered into the out skirts of Douglas and immediately saw a Motel 6. *That's the place for me!* Pulling into the entrance, I stopped at the office. In ten minutes, I was in my room. Opening the suitcase that contained my over-night items, I was soon in my pajamas, took two Melatonin, placed my head on my pillow and waited for a good night's rest.

***

The cellphone alarm woke me at 7 a.m. After showering and some facial make-up, I wore the same clothes bought at Walmart. As I walked down the hallway to the dining room, I met several couples who were leaving. I asked, "How is the breakfast menu?"

One lady stopped before me. "Excellent choices. I like your fall outfit. Most becoming."

"Thank you for the compliment, and recommendation for a good breakfast."

I picked up a plate and started to chow down. Very appetizing.

Finishing breakfast, I returned to my room, packed my suitcase and headed for the car. When walking between my car and the one beside me, I saw a pair of Montana issued plates on the pavement. As I picked them up, the owner of the car beside me said, "Oh, you found my plates I removed. Living in Wyoming now, I had to buy new plates. Too far to Billings to get back a refund. Have a good day." The man popped into his car, backed up, and drove away.

I looked at the plates again. *Positive all-points bulletin issued by Colorado. Stop me. Dare putting these on my car? Use till in Montana. Buy their plates.* I opened the trunk and found a screw driver in a tool box with other tools my ex-husband had collected. I had difficulty with one screw that was rusted tight. But I did get the Colorado plates off and replaced with Montana plates. I slid the Colorado plates under the floor mat, closed the door, got in, backed up, and headed for I-25. *Hope not stopped with these plates. A gamble.*

I drove a short distance and noticed my gas gauge was less than one-fourth. I pulled into the first gas station I saw and filled the tank. I went into the station and started to give the clerk my credit card. *Whoa! Can't use that!* I paid cash and, while waiting for the change, I picked up a brochure about the Wyoming Pioneer Memorial Museum. Featherlegs Monument, Stagecoach Museum and the Fort Fetterman Historic Site. *Hum-m. No big hurry. Enjoy the area history. Stay several days in Douglas.*

I spent four days visiting places in the area. It was really worth my time. I drove back to the motel late afternoon and shared my experiences with the desk clerk. I needed the rest and decided to sleep late every morning before visiting the various places.

CHAPTER 7

DIXIE

After eating breakfast, I packed my suitcase and placed it in the trunk. I entered my car. *Certain all-points bulletin out for car. I-25 crawling with patrolmen.* I googled a map of the area. *Secondary 59 and 14 go to Sheridan. Slower but safer.*

I found my way to No. 59. I discovered the road to be in much better condition than I expected. I saw a speed limit sign. *Darn heavy foot. Keep the limit. Patrolmen watching for speeders.*

I soon found myself driving through Thunder Basin National Grassland. I was so pleased I took this route for the scenery. It was absolutely beautiful. Signs for camp grounds were everywhere. Since I was not equipped to do any camping, I just kept heading north.

I reached Sheridan late afternoon. My gas gauge was showing almost empty. Pulling into the first gas station, I filled my tanks, paid cash, with plans to take I-90 to Billings. *Will be late. Best reserve room.*

I googled the motels in Billings. Wow! Over 40 to choose from. Vegas Hotel appears inviting. I found the telephone number and soon had a room reserved. When the person asked for a credit card number, I panicked. "I want to pay cash, ma'am!"

"I understand. That's fine. We just need a credit card to reserve your room. We don't run your card for payment."

I was relieved. "I'll be there late. How will I get my key?"

"No problem." The office is open 24/7."

"Good. I appreciate knowing that."

I wheeled out of the gas station to I-90. Just a short end in Wyoming, then Montana. *Here I come.*

CHAPTER 8
WYOMING HIGHWAY PATROLMAN NICK SHANNON

I was in my usual hiding spot right outside the city limits of Sheridan. It's an excellent place to catch drivers who begin accelerating to 40 or faster when the speed limit is posted at 30. But since I received the all-points bulletin to check every blue Subaru Legacy with Colorado plates, I was busier than usual. Didn't realize there are so many blue Subarus on the road.

I had already stopped seven Subarus since coming on duty. All checked out okay. I was leisurely eating a ham sandwich with my thermos of coffee at my side. "Oh, darn, there goes another blue Subaru."

"Here I go again!" I slipped my half-eaten sandwich in a baggie and screwed the cap tight on my thermos. I pulled out to I-90. "I'll just move behind the Subaru to check the plates. If not Colorado, I'll go back to my spot again," I said to myself.

***

Dixie saw the patrol car inching up behind her. *Damnit! I've had it! Plates won't match registration. Need to bite the bullet. So close to Montana. Murder trial. Prison. Horrible!*

***

I saw the Montana plates. She's just headed for home. No need to stop her.

***

I kept watching my rear-view mirror. *Not stopping me? Can't believe!* I continued watching. He slowed down, crossed over to the south bound lane and disappeared in the distance.

"Phew! That was far too close for comfort!" I said out loud. *Glad change plates. Would've been stopped. Arrested. Returned to Aurora.*

I drove to Billings. I googled the location of the Vegas Hotel. It was easy to find. *Thanks for little favors!*

The office attendant was most cordial. She gave me my keys and directed me to my room. In no time at all, I was "sawing logs"—perhaps, for me, "small branches."

CHAPTER 9
TOBY AND HIS FAMILY

Toby tapped his glass to get everyone's attention. "Do you realize that this is the third year that our family has met for noon dinner every Sunday? Imitating the ideas of the BLUEBLOODS' TV series is a really cool thing."

As the food dishes were being placed on the table, Toby glanced lovingly at each person who had made his life so meaningful—his mother and dad, Greta and Henry Rodriquez. who adopted him as a baby; his step-sister, Lucille, and her husband, Michael Dorsey. "Mother, would you tell me again later today how my birth mother abandoned me as a baby and you raised me along with Lucille?"

Greta looked at Toby with a smile. "Son, I have told you the story before. I will write out the full story in great detail so you can read it as many times as you desire. Is that okay with you?"

"Mother, that would be super. When I am eighteen in one month, can we try to find my dad and mom? That would be so much fun to know them."

Greta looked at her husband. "Toby, I've said it before, I haven't heard from my sister's whereabouts since she left me to baby-sit you. That is over 17 years ago, now. Your father left your mother before you were born. Might be difficult to find any trails."

Toby took a sip of water. "There are agencies or persons who make a living tracking down lost relatives. Maybe, we could find such persons that do researching."

"Henry, Dear. As a family counselor and divorce lawyer, do you have such contacts?"

"Not off hand. I have heard of such individuals or agencies. I'd have to do some research to find such people."

Toby punched Mike's shoulder. "You're a detective! Can you help to find my parents?"

"Toby, do you take me for a wizard? I can't find the name of the woman who may have killed her husband!"

"Hey, everyone. Let's say grace and eat before the food gets any colder," Greta said. "Toby, your turn to say grace."

Toby started saying the Lord's prayer. He heard everyone joining him.

Dishes of food were passed around. "I'm really starved!" said Toby. "I only had a glass of orange juice before we went to church. Paster Bob certainly had a meaningful sermon. He said that everyone needs to decide personally whether you want eternal salvation or eternal damnation before you die. I hope I didn't embarrass any of you when I joined the other four people in front of the sanctuary and received Jesus as my personal Savior?"

Greta reached for Toby's hand. "We are proud of you, Toby, for making the decision that we all have done already. You will never regret making that life-changing decision."

Toby laid his fork down. "Mike, you haven't learned the lady's name yet. Have you tried to contact someone in the office building she came out of when being grabbed by, I suppose, her husband?"

Mike dropped his fork on his plate. "Toby, you're brilliant! Why didn't I think of that connection in reviewing all the other facts and evidence so far."

Toby looked at Mike." I don't know why either. Perhaps, you didn't look outside the box for evidence, as the expression goes."

"I'm going there first thing tomorrow morning. At last, I might get a name to this elusive lady. Toby, you were certainly at the right place at the right time to find Dan Austin shortly after his death."

CHAPTER 10
DETECTIVE MICHAEL

I entered the office building two minutes after they opened. I realized it was a financial service type of business and went to the receptionist's desk.

"May I help you?"

"Yes, I'm Detective Michael Dorsey with the APD. Do you remember a lady wearing a white skirt and yellow blouse who was here last week Friday?"

"Indeed, I do. That would be Dixie Tallman. Loves bright colors. She worked here. That's her empty desk. I'll check if Sam Stevens can see you. He handled her account as personal advisor."

She dialed his office number. "There's a Detective Dorsey with APD who wishes to speak to you regarding Dixie."

Almost immediately, Sam arrived from his office and offered his right hand to Michael. "Come to my office, Detective."

***

"How can I help you?"

"Your receptionist called her Dixie Tallman. Can you provide more information about her? We need to find her in connection with the death of Dan Austin."

"Death? That's awful! That would be her ex-husband. They had a divorce around three years ago. Dixie resumed her maiden name of Tallman. She also worked for me until last Friday when she turned in her resignation. Efficient secretary. Indicated that she wanted to see the world! Since you are solving a death, I can break confidentiality rules. He was one mean hombre. One restraining order after another. No one could please him. Stalked her something fierce. Angry over the divorce settlement of the judge awarding her $90,000. We were handling her account with funds in escroll. However, she had spent $10,000 already and withdrew the $80,000 in cash, all in one-hundred-dollar bills. I told her the dangers of having that amount of cash on her person or in her house. She risked the danger of being robbed, or even murdered. Dixie is strong-willed and most adamant in her actions. We arranged with the bank for the funds and she left with the money in a sturdy valise last Friday."

"Do you have an address for her?"

"Yes, we do." I opened my computer to her account. "I'll write the address on my business card. If we can be of further help, call me."

"Thank you. You've been an enormous help already."

***

I trotted to my car. Pulling out my cellphone, I punched in the number for the DMV. "This is Detective Michael Dorsey with the APD. May I have the vehicle description for Dixie Tallman, address is" I pulled the business card from my shirt pocket, "1428 Semele Street. Apartment 2, Aurora."

I waited anxiously. "For a Dixie Tallman, we have a blue 2018 Subaru Legacy, Colorado plate number, NRS409. Do you need the VIN number?"

"No, not now. Thanks for the information."

***

I drove to my office as quickly as possible. Here I initiated an all-points bulletin to all law enforcement offices in Colorado and of the adjoining states. *If driving, might be lucky.*

***

I drove to the address for Dixie. I rapped on the door that read, "Office."

"Hello, I'm Helen. Can I help you? We do have vacancies."

"Yes. I'm Detective Michael Dorsey. I'm looking for a Dixie Tallman. She resides here, doesn't she, Apartment 2?"

"She did live here. She left a note under my door before she left." I opened my desk and pulled out the note and handed it to the detective.

I read it out loud and handed it back. "Did you know her well? Chit chats? Coffee together? Did she say anything about wanting to travel, assuming that may be the case?"

"Oh yes, indeed. Dixie had a wanderlust soul. A big one!"

Did she ever say where she wanted to travel?"

"Well, she did have a desire to see the major places in the U.S. She talked about flying to Paris, visit all parts of that country, then move to Great Britain, Germany, Switzerland, Italy and Israel. Then she said, if money didn't run out, China, and Japan. Also go live on one of the Hawaiian Islands. Good luck finding Dixie."

"You have been of great help, Helen, I think. She could be anywhere with what you shared. Here's my card. Please call me if you hear from Dixie."

"I'll certainly do that, Detective."

I drove back to my office slowly, my brain trying to digest all what I knew about Dixie. *Where on this earth can she be?*

CHAPTER 11
TOBY

"What the hell are you doing sitting at OUR table! Get your sorry ass out of here! Now!" yelled Herb Reston.

"I don't see your name of this table!" Kenneth shot back.

"Oh, a smart ass too boot! Get out of here before I pull that tongue of yours out through your asshole!"

I was sitting at the next table in the high school cafeteria. I jumped up and walked fast to the commotion at the table. "Take it easy, Herb. Don't blow a gasket! Must be some reason why he's sitting at your table." Looking at the student, "Who are you? Is this your first day here?"

"Yes, I'm Kenneth Clarkson. This is my first day. We just moved to Aurora. My dad was transferred to the Buckley Air Base."

"See, Herb, you jumped to a horrible conclusion. He didn't know the sitting arrangement here at Mitchell High. You owe Kenneth an apology."

"Sorry, Kid, for jumping down your throat!"

Kenneth stood up, looked into Herb's eyes and put out his right hand. "I accept your apology. Your threats don't scare me one bit."

Herb, not used to this type of response, put his hand out half-heartedly and shook Kenneth's. He quickly sat down, picked up a carrot stick from his tray and starting chewing it.

"Kenneth, pick up your tray and join my pals and me. Our table is a sort of free for all. The students here at Mitchell have a habit of sitting in the cafeteria by interest groups. The table we just left is for the Demos. The full name they use is Demolition. They are part of a street gang. A rival gang sits on the opposite side of the cafeteria and called the Ambassadors. They hate each other's guts, believe me. The tables on our left continues with two for the football team, then one table each for basketball team, the baseball, the track, and swimming. If you do any of these sports, you will be welcomed."

"I might just do that." said Kenneth. "Get to know more friends."

"The tables on our right are the pep squad and cheer leaders. Today is Friday and we have our first game tonight. We have a pep assembly this afternoon. The table next to us is the Geek Squad for all are in electronic classes. There are tables for the many clubs, organizations and interest groups like band, orchestra and choirs. Interesting how this has evolved. Sort of like the saying, birds of a feather, flock together."

Kenneth and I sat down. "Kenneth, this is Rocky Nelson, 185 pounds of solid muscle and plays tackle on our team. This is Slim Grabinski, one of our centers on the basketball team and plays end position on football team. I do football, baseball, track, and swimming. Do you do any sports?"

"Yes, I did all the sports at my last high school, except football. Sorry, Rocky, I don't prefer to have my brains bouncing around in my noggin. I do my best in baseball, however."

"What are your stats?" asked Toby.

"Last year, I averaged .32, 14 home runs, and 24 RBI's."

"Wow! Toby exclaimed. "Our baseball coach will go bonkers having you on the team. I have a dismal .19, 1 home run and 3RBI's."

We all started eating and a period of silence rolled over our table.

Toby broke the silence. "Kenneth, when I introduce you to. . ."

"Please call me Ken. My dad is Kenneth."

"Okay, Ken. As I was about to say, when I introduced you to Slim and Rocky, you folded your hands and slightly bowed. Are you into martial arts?"

"Yes, I have earned black belt level."

"Hear that Slim, Rocky? We are all black belt, too. This is really something! The students and faculty call us the 'Three Musketeers'. Somehow, it seems we are at the right place at the right time to help put out squabbles between students, sometimes even a fight or two. With black belt movements, we can put anyone on their back in no time. If you like, you can join us, if okay with Slim and Rocky, and we can be the Four Musketeers."

Both Rocky and Slim chimed in," Okay with me."

"I accept the offer," said Ken. "First day of school and I'm welcomed by three new friends. That was a great concern for me in attending a new high school."

"Slim, Rocky and I have been pals since the fifth grade. We've spent a lot of time together through the years-- studying, going to movies, hunting, skating, and just hanging out together at each other's homes, playing chess, checkers, video games, and card games. Our parents join us many times. Do you think your folks would object to three of us coming to your home?"

"I think my folks will be okay with that. I had friends over to my house back in Indiana where we lived."

Mitchell from the Geek Squad came and sat beside Toby. "Can you help me with a problem?"

"Musketeers, this is Mitchell from the next table. If you have any problems or repairs with your TV, computer, laptop, or cellphone, bring it to the Electronic Department. They repair for free and you pay parts only. Now what's your problem, Mitchell?"

"Two guys on the football team are forcing me to pay them my lunch money every day this week. You guys help a lot of students. Can you have them stop bullying me?"

"You bet we can, Mitchell. Who are they?"

"I don't know their names for sure. One I think is called Roger, but I can point them out to you."

"Let's go to the football table. You point out who the two guys are. We will do the rest to stop their bullying!" said Toby.

The Musketeers and Mitchell walked near the football table. "It's the two sitting together on the end of the table," as Mitchell pointed them out.

Toby put his hand on Mitchell's shoulder. "Go back and finish your lunch. We'll take over from here."

Toby and his pals went and stood behind Roger and Skeeter. Toby tapped both of them on their shoulders.

"What do you need, Toby?" asked Roger.

"I don't want anything right now. But, is that lunch you're eating now paid by the money you bullied Mitchell to give you?"

"Did he tell you that we asked for his money?" asked Skeeter.

"I believe you just admitted you did ask him. We are here to collect what he has paid you this week. Now!" demanded Toby.

"What if we don't want to pay it back? What can you do about it?" asked Roger.

"Well, let's see what we can do," said Toby. "How about telling Coach Jordan of your bullying habits and ask him for you two to do six laps around the football field."

"That's black mail!" exclaimed Roger. His outburst drew the attention of the other players.

"No, that's not black mail. It is called physical conditioning— more strength to play football," added Rocky.

"Don't tell the coach!" pleaded Roger. "We'll pay back every dollar."

"Okay. Bring the money to me next week without fail. Mitchell will be happy and also his parents. And no more bullying!" added Toby. He heard the other players snickering.

The Musketeers returned to finish their lunch.

"Can I introduce you to Coach Pete Callahan, our baseball coach?" asked Toby.

"Thanks, Toby. I have letters from my two former coaches. I prefer to approach the coach, look him in the eye, stick out my paw and introduce myself."

"Okay, Ken, the direct kind of offense! Oh joy, the bell," said Toby. "We always meet at the flag pole after school, unless we have practice. Tonight, is our first game. Rocky, Slim and I will be busy tonight. Well, Rocky and Slim will be. I may be keeping the bench warm. Ha.ha. Hope you can make it to the game"

CHAPTER 12
DETECTIVE MICHAEL

The Rodriquez family was meeting for their Sunday dinner at Michael and Lucille's home.

During the course of the meal, Mike shared a problem in his work. "We believe the couple that is renting the house at 1413 Cherry are members of a drug cartel. We think their names are Lisa and Carl Falcon. We have had fake utility trucks parked on the street, trying to get pictures of them or of their car plates to help make a more positive I.D. They never leave the house. A man, a butler, lives with them. The DMV ran his plates on his car. His name is Carl Batron."

"Have you gone to the house and ring the doorbell?" asked Toby.

"Yes, we have done that. The butler always answers the door. He apparently does all the shopping, too. He has been followed several times and provides no leads. Other detectives have tried starting a conversation with him, but he won't talk. Just grins and goes on his merry way. We have gone to the extent of going through their trash after the utility truck has picked up their garbage. Nothing that was useful. We went to the assessor office. But they are renting so they don't own the property. Blind alley!"

"Mike, the four Musketeers will put our brains in gear and figure out how to get the information you need," said Toby.

"Okay, Toby. Be my guest! Good luck. Let me know if you find out who these people are."

CHAPTER 13

THE FOUR MUSKETEERS

Toby went out to the patio, sat down and placed his feet on the fire pit ring.

I texted the rest of the Musketeers if free for the rest of Saturday morning to help solve the mysterious couple living in the house at 1413 Cherry Street. If free, I'll be around to pick you up.

I'm lucky to work part time as much as possible as a stock employee at an Ace Hardware Store. I had purchased a 2016 Honda Accord with my earnings last year. Well, my dad did contribute a tad. I didn't wait long, before all returned a text indicating each was free to help solve the mystery.

We arrived at my sis' house at 10 a.m. She was home for she doesn't work on Saturdays as a paralegal at a law firm. I rang the doorbell. She welcomed us in.

"Oh, you have added a fourth person to the Musketeers?' asked Lucille.

"Yes, this is Ken Clarkson, a new student at Mitchell. He is a black belt and we invited him to be a part of our group. His dad is stationed at Buckley Air Base," replied Toby.

"Welcome Ken. You've found some super friends."

"I'm the lucky one, Mrs. Dorsey."

"Call me Lucille, Ken. I'll get some snacks and drinks for you guys. I know you're trying to find out who are neighbors might be."

We went to the basement and surrounded a table. We sat and stared at each other.

"Does anyone have any ideas, crazy or not, how to solve the problem we have?" asked Toby.

"It seems obvious that we need to get the garage door open, and take a picture of the cars with license plate numbers before the residents know we did it. We know it's a two-car garage. Then some logical excuse as to why the garage door opened," contributed Ken.

The silence was so thick that it could be sliced.

"Does your sister have an extra garage opener?" asked Slim, breaking the silence.

"I'll go up and ask her," replied Toby. I climbed the steps to the kitchen, two at a time. "Sis, do you have an extra garage opener?"

"I believe there is one in the junk drawer at the end of the cabinet. We haven't used it since we moved in. May need new batteries," said Lucille.

I found it and pushed the button and heard the garage door open. "Works great, sis!"

I hit the button again and heard the garage door close as I bounded down the steps to the basement. "It works!" I laid it on the table. "Now what.?"

Slim picked it up. "Guys, I have a brain storming idea. Toby, didn't you say that you watched all the houses being built after this house was finished?"

"Yeah. The same construction company did all five houses," added Toby.

Slim opened the device and studied the code numbers. "This opener has a code of 653211. Let's say the builder was smart, and installed the same make of garage doors in each garage, but was lazy and only changed the last digit for each house. The 1413 house might have a code of 653215. I'll change the one to a five. Toby, do you have a football in your car?" asked Slim.

"Yes, but what does the football have to do with the opener?" asked Toby.

Slim snapped the cover on the opener. "The four of us can go down the street, tossing the football between us. When we get to 1413, I'll press the button in my pocket."

"Ah, yes! I got the picture!" exclaimed Toby. "If the door opens, I'll quickly take a picture of the car or cars. I'm sure whoever lives there, will come out the house wondering about the open garage door."

"Will just keep tossing the football as though passing by the house," said Rocky.

"What if they stop us and ask questions or get angry?" asked Slim.

"Good point," said Toby.

Ken jumped up. "I know what to say. I've heard of cars passing by a house with the radio or CD player turned up blasting away and the vibrations met the frequency of the door opener. We can use that explanation if needed."

"Might work, Ken. Worth a shot if needed," said Toby.

The Musketeers met on the sidewalk, two going out in the street. They threw the football to each other as they walked or ran. In front of 1413, Slim activated the opener in his pocket. Sure enough, the door opened. Toby had his cellphone ready and snapped a picture of the two cars. Pocketing his cellphone quickly, he threw the football that Rocky had tossed to him. As predicted, a man and woman came rushing out of the house with the other man looking out of the house door.

"Did you kids open the damn garage door?" demanded the man that might be Carl Falcon "Oh, no sir, I didn't," responded Toby. "We were just throwing the football to each other. A car did go by with its wolfers and tweeters blaring away. The vibration must had triggered your door opener mechanism. We were surprised too when the garage door opened."

The suspected Carl Falcon looked at his door opener in his hand. "Could be what happened. I've heard of airplanes flying over houses that triggered garage openers. Do you young men live around here.? Haven't seen you around."

"No, Mr. Falcon. My sister and her husband live up the street four houses." Toby pointed his hand in the direction. "My sister invited us to her house for snacks and drinks after we threw the football to each other for some time. We are seniors at Mitchell

High and all play on the football team except Ken." Toby laid a hand of Ken's arm. "That's why we were practicing throwing and catching as we were going by your house."

"Please to meet you young men. You appear to be well mannered. But my name is not Falcon. Don't know where you got that name. I'm Jerry Mathias and my wife is Judith. Our butler watching us from the door is Carl Batson.

Toby pointed to the cars. 'Two Porches! Wow! They are neato!"

"Yes, the red one is mine and the yellow is Judith's. We drove these here from Chicago where I was working. I was transferred, what, three months ago?" He looked at his wife.

"It's closer to four months now, Dear," shared Judith.

"Time flies! We haven't driven them since. My work is all done on my computers, cellphone and sometimes on the land phone. Our butler does all the shopping. Judith, we should drive them just to keep the batteries charged." Jerry closed the garage door. "Need to get back to work. Judith and I are pleased to meet you young men. Have a great football season and win the trophy!"

"Thanks, Mr. Mathias. We will do our very best with the rest of the team," said Toby.

The Musketeers returned to Toby's sister's house, throwing the football along the way.

Sitting around the table in the kitchen eating snacks and drinking canned drinks, Toby exploded, "We did it! Wow! Awesome!" I pulled out my cellphone and sent the picture of the cars to Mike's phone number. Next, I texted the real names—Jerry and Judith Mathias. Butler is Carl Batson.

"Mike will surely appreciate the detective work of the Musketeers," said Lucille.

"Yup!" replied Toby, "We were all in the right place at the right time to help Detective Mike."

CHAPTER 14
DETECTIVE MICHAEL

I sat in my office contemplating why no reports had come in from any highway patrolmen having stopped Dixie. *Lucky! Driving secondary roads? Smart Cookie. Will slip up. Somewhere. Some time!*

I needed to find out if Dixie had any violation of using a gun in the past. I opened my computer and search the public records, criminal records and arrest records. I found nothing listed for a Dixie Tallman or Dixie Austin.

Next, I entered Dan Austin. Bingo! He had a record of illegal possession of three grams of cocaine and two ounces of marijuana seven years ago. Two guns found in glove compartment. One a .22 Smith and Wesson pistol- -Serial number 218-41127. Another gun-- .45 Ruger pistol—Serial number 142-42346. Has Nonprofessional Permit to carry weapons. Permit number 105XMB35 issued 03/11/2018. Expiration date 03/11/2023. Dan must have given the .22 to Dixie before the divorce. *So much for that.*

Typing out a profile of Dixie with the information I already knew, I determined she would be in desperation of the gun being found on her person. She has already disposed of the gun. But how? Where?

I drove back to her former resident. Rapping on the manager's door, Helen opened the door with a large smile on her face.

"Oh, hello Detective. Back so soon?"

"Yes. Are her rooms still the same? No cleaning? No dumping of her possessions?"

"No, Detective. I have been too busy visiting my sister who needs a lot of attention with her health issues. I haven't been able to clean the rooms for new rentals."

"It's fortunate for me that you haven't. Here is the search warrant approved by Judge Vincent. May I have a key and go through her rooms with a fine-tooth comb? May find a clue or two to her whereabouts."

I found the bedroom in disarray. It was obvious that she packed in a big hurry. Starting with her desk, I searched every nook and cranny. I did find two envelopes with the return address from two people—one living in New York City and the other in Bristol, Massachusetts. I took out my notepad and jotted down the names and addresses. I need to write both to determine if she contacted them within the week. *Driving that far? Possibly? Not probable.*

Doesn't fit profile. I examined the pockets of the clothes on the bed and in her closet *Nothing.*

I found that she didn't have any miscellaneous items or clutter anywhere in her closet, the kitchen cupboard or the drawers. *Fits her profile.* I found nothing to help determine her whereabouts, except the letters from her friends or relatives on the East coast.

I returned to my office. Opening my computer, I composed a letter to the two persons who had corresponded with Dixie. I requested that they contact me immediately if she arrived at their places or contacted by phone or email. *Worth the effort.*

CHAPTER 15
TOBY

I jumped out of bed when my cellphone alarm started buzzing. I had to be at work at the hardware store. I had a text from my boss indicating that a large amount of merchandise had been delivered. That meant a lot of work, but that's what I'm paid to do.

The first boxes I wheeled to the paint department were quarts of interior paints. As I was pushing these cans on the shelves by color, I heard one can tipping over and rolling to the back of the shelf. I'm too short to reach over six feet to retrieve the can, so I walked to the maintenance room for a step ladder.

Stepping up two rungs to reach the can, I saw a gun behind the paint cans I had just pushed on the shelf. *Who put it there? How long ago?*

I jumped off the ladder to find Mr. Johnson, my boss and owner of the store. Finding him in his office, he followed me to the place. He climbed the ladder two steps and witnessed what I had seen.

"We need to call the police, Toby. Why not call your brother-in-law?"

Since it was 8:30 a.m., I first called him at his home. Lucille told me that he had just left for his office, even though it was Saturday, his day off. I called his cellphone and caught him driving.

"Mike, I found a revolver that looks like a .45 caliber laying on the shelf behind the paint cans at Ace Hardware. Can you come or call your officer buddies to get here?"

"Which hardware store do you work at, Toby?"

"It's the one on 600 block of Peoria."

"I'm on my way. Probably 10 minutes out. I'll use my siren to help."

I saw Michael pull up in front of the store and went out to meet him. "You made good time!"

"Lead the way, Toby, to the paint department."

***

"I should put on my gloves, first," said Michael. I climbed up the two steps on the ladder. I removed the gun and started to bag it. "We have a murder victim in the morgue now that was killed with a .45 revolver. We have the bullet from the forensic lab. Will be interesting if it matches this gun."

Another Aurora policeman arrived as Michael was placing the gun in a plastic container. "Sargent, would you please run this gun to our forensic lab for any fingerprints and ask them to do a ballistic I.D to the bullet removed from the victim, Dickey Holliday, two weeks ago."

***

Mr. Johnson had been watching Detective Michael bagging the gun. "Detective, we do have a security system. We have five security cameras in key spots. The system records for three weeks. If we don't stop it, the system recycles, deleting the previous pictures. This is the end of three weeks tomorrow. If the person placing the gun behind the paint cans was during the last three weeks, there may be pictures of the person."

"Great! Can I view it now or can I take the recordings to our lab and record it to our system for reviewing?" asked Michael.

"Yes, you may take it with you. I'll get the recordings for you now."

"Toby, if the system recorded for three weeks, and the murder was two weeks ago, it is feasible that this might be the weapon used. At least the time frame coincides."

"Here are the recordings, Detective. I hope the images will be the help you need."

"Thank you, Mr. Johnson. Toby, guess you can go back to work. Just don't find any more guns. But you certainly were in the right place at the right time, once again."

CHAPTER 16

DIXIE

I was awakened by someone rapping on my door. "Housekeeping!" Jumping out of bed, I walked rapidly to the door and flipped the security bar. Opening the door a crack, "Sorry, I slept late and I'm not ready for the day. No need to clean my room for I plan to be here several days."

"Okay Ma'am. Here are clean towels and wash cloths."

I took the offered items. "Thank you. Great service."

I grabbed the notepad and pencil on the night stand, and jumped back into bed. I started my to-do-list.

1. Dixie Tallman name needs to disappear.
2. Dye hair as a brunette.
3. Find street person who can provide a source to get a driver's license.
4. Change name to Elsie Mae Dole. Address yet to be determined. How to do it.
5. Sell Subaru, No title or registration form? How?
6. Buy different car.
7. Check each of the small towns to find one that is inviting or suitable.
8. Find motel in small town to live temporarily.
9. Rent a post office box number in town selected.
10. Find an apartment in small town selected.
11. Check gift shops for crafts selling best.

12. Get new driver's license.
13. Buy new license plates.

I had unpacked my suitcases and hung up my clothes before going to bed. *Really wrinkled. What the heck! Casual look.* I selected a long sleeve beige blouse and a pair of Demin jeans and slipped into them. I grabbed my valise and placed it in the safe that was bolted to the floor in my closet. Selecting a combination number, I closed the door. *Hope it's safe.* I slipped into my flats, picked up my purse and a light gray jacket and left, making certain the door was locked. When I reached the lobby, I realized I was hungry—very hungry. *Hotel restaurant? Find another place?*

Reaching the parking lot, I found my car sandwiched between two utility vans that apparently arrived after I had parked. There was no space for me to get into my car. I tried to side step between vehicles, but the door could not be opened to slide in. I went to the office attendant and told her my dilemma.

"Oh, the linemen are eating breakfast. Go in and ask one to move their van."

I went to the dining room. Pouring a cup of coffee, I sat at a table beside the two men.

"Good morning. Do you two purposely place a maiden in distress or is it just accidental?"

"Good morning to you, too! But for you to unload such an accusation so early in the day seems unnecessary, especially when I don't know what the hell your problem is," answered the man with curly black hair.

"Well, you parked your vans so close to my car that I can't even squeeze in between or open my door."

"For Pete's sake, woman. You're making a mountain out of a mole hill. Follow me and I'll back my van out so you can be on your way."

"I'm not in any hurry. Can we finish our coffee first?"

"Okay, lady. We're not in a hurry either."

"The name is Elsie Mae."

"Now were being civil. I'm Bob and this is my side kick, Roberto."

"Pleased to meet you both. Where do you do all your utility work?"

"We're finishing a new telephone line in the Laurel area serving nine smaller communities."

"I saw those small town on my googled maps. I am also new to Montana. Which of those nine communities would be the most inviting for me to consider moving to?"

Bob looked at Roberto. "Hard to say, Elsie Mae. The largest town is Bridger and has many amenities. We usually stay at the Quality Inn Motel each night while working in the area, but we had to come to Billings for more equipment and supplies."

"Thank you for that information. I had planned to drive to each and case the joint, as the expression goes. You have saved me much time. I'll drive to Bridger to find housing."

"Glad we can be of help, Elsie Mae. Ready for us to move our rigs? We need to be on our way to Bridger now to finish our work."

The men and their vans left. I entered my car, took out my purse, found my to-do-list and crossed out No. 7. Now I need a new I.D. I drove slowly on several streets. Spotting a likely person that appeared to be living on the streets, I parked and walked to where he was leaning against a building, one foot on the wall and chewing on a match stick.

"Excuse me, sir. Are you in the know of a source in Billings that can make ID cards and driver license?"

"Could be, lady. How much is it worth to you?"

"I don't know what the going rate might be."

"Well now, since I am short on cash, I'll make a discount of $200."

"That much? How about the source to make the ID cards."

"Probably in the area of $800."

"That is a lot more than I expected."

"My source does excellent work. Can't tell his work from the real ones."

"I need to think about that expense. Thanks for the help." I opened my purse and pulled out a twenty-dollar bill. "Do you stay in this area of Billings so I can find you again?"

"Yup! This is my office area. I can help anyone-- at any time— even the police come to me."

I retuned to my car and drove back to the hotel. I saw the computer room. I googled "Montana legal name change." Up popped a legal form with Total Legal. Filling out the information requested, I clicked on "continue." This led me to more needed information. I waited impatiently one week while a judge approved my name change and to be mailed to the hotel address.

During the time I was waiting for my legal name change, I had accomplished more items on my to-do-list. I had asked Priscilla at the registration desk for the name of her beauty salon. After making an appointment, I became a brunette.

I had exchanged the Montana plates for the Colorado ones. I knew I was taking a chance of being caught, not knowing how wide a territory the all-points bulletin had been sent.

I had gone to Bridger and had driven up and down the streets to see the amenities the town had to offer. I saw the necessary places I would need. I found the Quality Inn motel and made reservations for the following week. The post office had been easy to find and rented a post office box.

I had gone to the DMV in Billings and asked for a booklet to study for acquiring a driver's license. After a day of studying, I had returned, took the written and vision test, which I passed. The driving test was not needed. In less than an hour, I had my temporary license with my new name. *All legal,* I mused to myself.

At the end of the week, the legal documents were waiting for me at the hotel address. I held the document at arm's length. I was so happy, tears rolled done my cheeks.

I drove to the Subaru dealer. As I drove on the lot, I spied a green Volkswagen. I drove to where it was parked. I read the written information on the windshield. "2000 Green Beatle. Good condition. $4,900. *That car has my name on it!* I drove back to the office and parked.

As I was getting out of my car, a salesman met me. "Well, lovely lady, how can I help you. I'm Edward?"

"I'm Else Mae. You can do two things for me. Appraise my car and give me the best price for that lovely Green Beatle."

"You wish to trade your 2018 Subaru for the 2000 Beatle?"

"Yes. I need the difference to help me with living expenses until I find a job." I hated telling a little white lie.

"I understand your problem. Let me get the person who appraises cars and we can then move on to the trade. Come with me to my office while he does his examination. I see that you have Colorado plates. Do you have a Montana driver's license?"

"I have a temporary one." I opened my purse and gave it to him.

"Great. Do you have the title to your car?"

"No, my dead ex-husband must have it in his property. We divorced three years ago and have been driving the car without the title or registration form. I think I have car insurance but nothing to prove I have it."

"That's not a huge problem. We have a form to fill out to get a title without the original one." He opened his desk drawer and handed the form to me to fill out. I did and returned it to him.

The evaluator stopped at Edward's door. "Her Subaru is in excellent condition with only 10,542 miles. Good tires. Motor sounds great. No slippage of the transmission. No dents or dings. Our offer is $20,000."

I sat up straight, gave a big sigh. "If I can buy the Beatle for $5,000, I would have $15,000 to live on."

"Elsie Mae, that's a trade we can arrange right now." He disappeared for some time, but came back with forms printed out with all the information. Edward gave me a pen and I signed my name to the places that were indicated by green arrow stickers.

We walked to the Beatle. Edward placed the temporary plates on it. "This car has 121,400 miles on it, three owners, and no accidents. You have a great car for years to come. We can have us service it for you when needed or go to the Volkswagen Dealership. That's your choice."

I entered my new car and rolled down the window. "Thank you, Edward. You're a great salesman." I stuck my right hand out the window and we shook hands.

"It's been a delight to help you, Elsie Mae."

"I'll see you within the month for service for my lovely green Beatle." I patted the dashboard lovingly.

"Best to you Elsie Mae. Look forward to seeing you again."

CHAPTER 17
ELSIE MAE DOLE

I drove out of the lot. I sensed a difference in driving my Beatle but I knew I would get used to the change. I drove to my hotel, care free, and not a worry in the world. How refreshing it is to be lost to everyone looking for me, yet I know exactly where I am.

Arriving at my room, I jumped on my bed, took out my to-do-list and crossed out everything that I had accomplished. I was glad that I had done everything legally. Before I would move to the motel in Bridger, I must get new license plates. Then find a couple of stores that sell crafts items.

The weather was chilly, so I changed to the khaki slacks, the brown blouse, and my classy jacket. I left the hotel and drove to the DMV. I took a number and waited my turn. It was most interesting watching people fidgeting and looking nervous; mothers trying to console their children who were tired of sitting still, and fathers apparently ignoring their children. Others were smart and were reading books. *Wonder what having children like? Glad I didn't. Make lousy mother.*

My number was finally called. I took a seat at Window five, gave the man all my paper work on my car. "I have your title and bill of sale, but I need your driver's license."

I dug it out of my billfold. "The license is only temporary. I haven't received the real one yet."

"It's all we need. Here are your plates. That will be $25.75."

"I trust you will take cash."

"No, problem, Elsie Mae."

I gave him a twenty and a ten. As she gave me my change, I asked "I'm new to Billings, so can you suggest the best gift shops."

"Why, yes, I can. I usually go to Spencer's or Joy of Living. Both have a large selection of items to choose from."

"Thank you. I do appreciate the information."

I went to my car. I googled the names she gave me and saved the addresses. I drove to Spencer's, parked, and walked to the store. As I entered, I immediately knew what the lady at DMV had said about selection. I looked over the factory produced items, but my eyes were drawn to a different item that appeared to be crafted by someone with great skills.

A clerk approached me. "May I help you?"

"Yes, these plaques intrigue me. They are different and so attractive."

"Yes, they are indeed. They are called Shaker Peg Plaques. The ones you see are the only ones left. The lady, Ann Reston, who lived in Bridger, made these. However, she died from COVID. She lived with her daughter, Priscilla Brunning whose husband also died of COVID."

"How terrible! Many lives were lost. I know of other friends and relatives that died from the epidemic. These plaques appear to be something I could do. I have done considerable amounts of crafting.

"These sell very well. She made a wide variety to compliment the décor of any room. The nursery items sold the best. Unfortunately, none are left. Here is a picture that Ann produced that shows all the different plaques she made. I used it many times for customers to select from and Ann would make a plaque to order. By the way, I am the owner of the store. My name is Margaret Finley."

"Pleased to meet you. I am Elsie Mae Dole. Do you have Priscilla's address so I might pay her a visit? I plan to find housing in Bridger. Right now, I will live at the Quality Inn."

"Yes, here is Ann's business card with the necessary information you need."

"This plaque with kitchen décor is really attractive. I wish to buy it."

"They sell for $30. Twenty was Ann's portion. She told me that it may cost around $5 to make a plaque. That gave her around $15 profit. Since her death, I have been sending that portion to Priscilla."

"That sounds fair enough. Here is $30. I shall visit Priscilla as soon as I arrive in Bridger. I hope that I can start producing these plaques for you as soon as possible."

"That would be an advantage for both of us. Here is a notepad to get your information."

I provided her with my necessary contact information. "Plan to see you soon, Margaret."

CHAPTER 18
SAM AND EDNA HOLDEN

"**S**am, I'm getting hungry. We have been driving too long a time since breakfast. Cheyenne is coming up soon by the sign we just passed. Can we stop to get a lunch?"

"Yes, my Dear. Google your cellphone for a good place to eat."

I did just that. But at that moment, we passed the Albany Hotel advertising sign. I'll try it. I googled the address and GPS had us there and we were sitting in a booth in no time.

"Edna, you did us great! That was an excellent lunch. It is early in the day, but we could stay here for the night."

"Have you forgotten, Dear. We made reservations in Rawlings for tonight. We have 150 miles to drive yet. Let's pay the bill and get moving."

We got to the car. "I can't find my keys!"

"Did you check all your pockets, Dear?"

I patted all my pockets. "No, I don't have them. Let's trace our steps back to the hotel and to the dining room. May have lost them along the way. They may even have found them and waiting for us to reclaim them."

We searched the pavement and then the hotel floor. We retraced our steps again. I went to the cashier. "Did you find a set of keys?"

"No, none were turned in." The manager led us back to the booth where we ate lunch. "I don't see any keys on the floor. Are you certain you didn't lose then outside?"

"No, we already checked the street and the lobby floor," said Sam.

The manager ran his hand along the back of the seat. "There is an open space I didn't know was there. Could your keys have fallen out of your pocket as you got into or out of the booth and they slipped through this space? Possible, isn't it? Sally, would you ask our maintenance man to bring a screw driver."

He arrived with his electric drill containing a Phillip head bit. He laid down on the floor and soon had the four screws backed out. Standing up, he lifted the seat from the box.

The manager looked down inside. "Yep! Here are your keys," as he reached in and gave them to Sam. "But there is also a gun: I wonder how long it has been there? I better call the police and have them removed it."

Sam dangled his keys. "Thanks for finding them. Best we be on our way."

CHAPTER 19
SERGEANT PATRICK MCDOWELL

I arrived at the Albany Hotel and stopped a waitress. "Had a call to the station and then sent to my squad car that you found a gun inside a seat. Strange message."

"Yes, it's true. I'll take you to the booth."

I looked down and saw the gun. I lifted my cap and scratched my head. "This is totally weird. Any idea how long it has been there?"

The manager approached the policeman. "Can you remove the gun so maintenance can replace the seat. Don't wish to excite the customers already here or new ones arriving."

"Yes, I can." I pulled a glove from my back pocket and slipped it on. I picked up the gun and held it against my leg, walked out to my car, slipped it in a plastic bag, and placed it under my car seat. When I returned to the restaurant, the seat was being replaced and fastened down. Again, I asked the manager if he had any idea how long the gun has been hidden in the seat.

"We replaced all the seat coverings three years ago. So, it could have been any time since."

"Okay. I'll write up my report accordingly." I left and returned to my precinct headquarters.

I opened my computer and wrote out my report:

> On October 1, 2022, a request was made by manager Joseph Collins, of the Albany Hotel,

Laramie, Wyoming, the discovery of a .22 Smith and Weston pistol Serial No. 218-41127, found inside a box seat. Possible concealment within the last three years. Person or persons placement is unknown.

After reviewing my report for accuracy, I placed it in Captain Ed Posa's in-basket. I retuned to my office to do another report before going out on patrol again. I was about to leave when Captain Posa came into my office with my report in his hand.

"That is an interesting report you gave me. Do you think the gun might have been used in a crime—murder perhaps?"

"Anything could be possible, Captain."

"May be wise to send an all-points bulletin to the major police precincts in Wyoming and to the neighboring states. Might get some results."

I left for the main office staff and gave them the report to have the necessary information for the all-points bulletin.

CHAPTER 20
DETECTIVE MICHAEL

I was lounging in my chair working on the various files of cases that were not solved as yet because of leads drying up. I picked up the five files and went to the office of Detective Andy next door.

"Andy, have you made any dent in these cases that are backing up on us?"

"No, I was just going through each of them. Brain-storming hasn't helped a darn bit. All I get is a headache."

"Yup! Know the feeling." I returned to my office.

Sally from the main office knocked on my door. "Come in,"

She held out a folder to me. "Detective Mike, you may be very interested in this all-points bulletin that just arrived."

I opened the folder and scanned it quickly. "Thanks Sally. Good information." She left.

I read it more carefully. I opened my computer to check if the serial numbers were the same as from the criminal record of Austin Hill. The same .22 caliber gun!

So, our "bird of flight" was in Laramie, Wyoming. Now, did she take I-80 to the West coast and fly to one of the Hawaiian Islands; or, I-80 East and then I-90 to New York or other air ports in the area to fly to Paris; or did she continue north on I-25 to some place in Wyoming or even Montana. I ruled out Canada for now

I opened Dixie's profile and added the new information and the possible whereabouts of her. Opening a map of Wyoming, I listed the possible places that I thought she might have considered as a place to live. I studied the list for some time.

Next, I opened the map of Montana and listed the possible place for her to find housing. For some reason, Billings just seemed to merge out above all the other cities and towns. It would be a large city in which to get lost if that were her objective. If Dixie selected Billings, where can I find any clues to her whereabouts. *Hotels? No. Motels? No. Over 40. Too many. Post office? No. Subaru dealer? More likely. Service car. Worth a try*

I googled Subaru dealership in Billings. Rimrock Subaru, address and telephone number showed up. I jotted down the phone of 406 651 5200 on Dixie's profile and dialed the number.

"Rimrock Subaru, how may I help you."

"This is Detective Michael Dorsey with the Aurora, Colorado Police Department.'

"Okay Detective. How can I help you?"

"Have you, per chance, serviced or traded a 2018 Blue Subaru Legacy with Colorado plates, The owner would be Dixie Tallman."

"Let me bring up service jobs on my computer. No, I have none for that name the last week."

"Is it possible that she sold the Legacy to you or maybe a trade?"

"I believe that did happen. Let me transfer you to Edward Samples who had a trade with a lady recently."

***

"This is Edward Samples. How may I help you?"

"This is Detective Michael Dorsey with the Aurora Colorado Police Department. I am trying to locate a lady by the name of Dixie Tallman, blonde, 5 feet 7 inches, who is or was driving a 2018 blue Subaru Legacy with Colorado plates number NRS409."

"Well, Detective, I did trade with a lady with that car description, but she was a brunette, about the same height. Her name, however, was Elsie Mae Dole."

"*Very interesting. Changed name? Not her profile.* Did she have an address?

"Let me bring that trade up on my computer. Ah, yes, it is P.O. Box 410, Bridger, 54910."

"Thank you. Did this Dole lady buy another car?"

"She traded the Legacy for a 2000 Beatle."

"How far is Bridger, is that the town you said, from Billings?"

"Yes, it is B-r-i-g-d-e-r. I would estimate 50 miles."

"Thank you, Edward, for the information."

"You're welcome, Detective. Hope you find your lady?"

***

I leaned back in my chair while running the conversation through my head. I had to make some sense out of all that information. Are there two different women: an Elsie Mae Dole that traded cars, a 2018 Subaru Legacy with Colorado plates and a Dixie Tallman with the same make of car somewhere in Wyoming and beyond. What are the odds to have identical cars but different Colorado plates? Did Dixie, in desperation, change her name? *Doesn't fit profile.*

Could be wrong. Done by judge. Too many to contact- verify. I closed the file. *Need cup coffee.*

CHAPTER 21

TOBY

I completed stocking the merchandise all morning and left by noon. Walking outdoors, I found the day was bright and sunny with a light cool breeze. Ah, yes, a perfect day to hunt grouse and rabbits, and also look for Indian arrow heads. Pulling out my cellphone, I texted my three buddies if free for the afternoon to go hunting. I knew Slim and Rocky had guns. I texted Ken separately regarding having a shot gun or rifle. If none, I would lend him one. He answered back that he could use his dad's .20 gauge. Slim and Rocky answered back that each was free, also.

I made the round in picking them up. I drove to the far east part of Aurora with wide stretches of undeveloped land. My dad and I had hunted in this area before. I parked on a driveway that was badly eroded with a gate that was normally well wired shut. As we approached the gate, we saw that all the wires were cut and the ends laying on the ground.

"Someone has gone through this gate. We have always climbed in between the wires," Toby said, which we all did.

"Is that a large patch of grass and two trees in the distance that are growing in this barren soil?" asked Ken.

"Yes," answered Toby. "There apparently is underground water seeping to the surface. See that ditch to our left? I would say that was a good running stream and an ideal place for Indians to have lived here 150 years or more ago. So, let's hunt for arrow heads that may have been uncovered by recent rains while walking to the hunting area."

Toby used his toe to scratch the dirt from a piece of rock sticking up through the ground. "Hey, guys. Come here. I believe this is a piece of an arrow, at least more than half."

The three came and surrounded Toby. "Yes. That has to be shaped by someone, "shared Slim, "The point is so obvious."

"That seems to be proof that some Indian group lived in this area. Let's spread out again and search some more. May find a whole arrow head," said Toby.

"Did you notice a lot of tire tracks in the soft dirt areas?" asked Ken.

"Yes, I did. Some hunters must have been too lazy to walk to this grassland," said Toby

We reached the tall grass that was turning brown from the fall weather. "Slim and Rocky, you walk along the edge of the grass. If rabbits come out, have at it. Ken and I, with shotguns, will walk through the grass to chase rabbits out for you and for us to get any grouse. Watch where you're shooting at all times, guys."

We walked very slowly, being alert to any movements in the grass. Toby saw a large mound of grass ahead of him. I stepped over it when my left foot landed on something soft. I brought my right foot across and stopped. Putting my gun on safety, I moved the grass away with the end of my gun. "Good grief! A hand!" I blurted out. "Hey guys, put your guns on safety and come here. There's a body under this bunch of grass!" Again, I used the end of my gun to move the grass from the face. It was a woman with her face covered with dried blood.

"Oh no! How terrible," screeched Ken.

Slim ran from the dead body and begin to toss his cookies. Toby had to swallow hard several times to stop the reflex of vomiting.

Toby pulled out his cellphone from his pocket. "Hope we have reception this far away to call Detective Michael." I touched his numbers.

"Detective Michael Dorsey. How may I help you?"

"Mike, this is Toby. Us guys were hunting east of Aurora, off of S. Conservatory Parkway and Greenwood Place. We found a dead woman covered with grass. Blood is very dry on her face. The body is between two small trees. There is a gate you can use to drive to the spot."

"Toby, we'll get the team out right away. But you guys leave immediately in the event who ever did this may come back for some reason. Drive some distance from there yet have sight of the road. If any activity before we arrive, call me."

"Okay, Mike. We'll do that. We're out of here."

"Guys, Mike wants us to scram immediately but drive down the road some distance so we still can see the gate. He thinks there is a possibility of the bad people coming here before the forensic team arrives."

We ran to the car, placed our guns in the trunk and drove around three-fourths of a mile down the road and parked. Opening the trunk of the car, I pulled out a pair of binoculars from a box of camping gear. They were perfect to watch the areas for any traffic. We took turns glassing the area.

We waited 35 minutes before we saw a line of five cars speeding down the road. Mike must have been first, as we watched him open the wire gate. The cars shot through and to the place of the body. Toby removed his cellphone from his pocket and touched the numbers for Mike's.

"Thanks Toby, for being our watch dog. We'll take over from here."

"I'm taking the guys home. So much for a dead body ruining our hunting spree."

"Some days are like that, Toby. But you guys were at the right place to find the body."

CHAPTER 22
TOBY AND FAMILY

It was another Sunday when the family met for dinner at the Rodriquez' home after attending church.

During the course of the meal, Mike shared what Toby had uncovered while hunting.

"Toby, again, you and your buddies were at the right place at the right time. There is no way of knowing how long the lady's body could have been hidden by the grass, The forensic team was greatly surprised that no wild animals had destroyed the body in the estimated time of one month. Flies of course, found the body, but the damages were minimal."

"How was she killed?" asked Toby

"Forensic determined she was shot in the stomach with a shot gun, and then a .45 caliber bullet to the forehead. It was an overkill. Forensic was very surprised the slug was still in her skull. A fluke. Normally the bullet exits the back of the skull. We searched through that tall grass for the shell casings but found nothing.

"What about the .45 I found at the store??" asked Toby.

"Toby, I was about to say that the .45 you found was the gun that killed the lady. Perfect match."

"Did the security camera from the store help any?" asked Toby

"No, Toby, unfortunately, we saw images of several men and women, but they were wearing those COVID masks. We couldn't identify anyone. There was no picture the camera caught of anyone placing the gun behind the paint cans."

"Did the tire tracks help any?" asked Toby.

"No, the dirt was too soft or too hard. No tire threads were visible to make cast."

"Would finding the shell casing and the spent gunshot tube help you or the Forensic team?"

"Might help. Sometimes there is a partial finger print on the shell casing when filling the magazine. We checked all the loaded shells and the magazine itself, but no prints."

"You'll catch them, Mike. Sooner or later!"

"Thanks, Toby. I'll do my best but we need some hard evidence to find the murderers."

"You realized, guys, that this topic is not the best to have at our dinner," said Lucille

"Sorry about that family. I know you all have strong stomachs, I hope," offered Mike.

CHAPTER 23
DETECTIVE MICHAEL

On a bright and early Monday morning, I was sitting with most of the Aroura Police Department officers for daily briefing. The captain shared the cases that were critical to be solved. Other problems of the street gangs were enumerated.

"Officers, we need to grind the dangerous individuals in our community to dust, so we can sweep them away. We are getting dozens and dozens of calls from our neighborhoods of the theft, murders, harassments, drive by shootings, home invasions and carjacking. For Heaven's Sake, when anyone finds a situation that needs attention and an arrest, please call for backup. Let's not have any John Wayne tactics and jump in the fray alone. You well know that we have placed too many to rest of late."

"Captain, are we acquiring any new officers or is there any action to defund our police force," asked Michael.

"No, we are not being defunded. However, we are able to add one more detective to your group of five to help solve the cases that are building up unsolved. The police commissioner wants results. I understand when leads dry up, but help each other with brain storming methods to come up with new leads or clues. Any other questions or statements? If not, go get them!"

***

Mike went to his office. He opened the file on Dixie. I need to find out if she and Elsie Mae are one in the same, or by coincidence, different ladies with the same kind of cars.

As I pondered on this problem, the light bulb effect took place. THE LICENSE PLATE NUMBERS! Why didn't I think of asking Edward Samples before? I'll call him again.

"Subaru Dealers. How may I help you?"

"Would you please connect me to Edward Samples. This is Detective Michael Dorsey with the Aurora Colorado Police Department."

"Yes, Detective. I remember your call from before. I'll connect you to his office."

***

"Edward Samples, speaking."

"Edward, this is Detective Michael Dorsey. We spoke earlier."

"Yes, Detective, regarding Elsie Mae Dole and the trade."

"Yes, when you take the plates off of cars you buy or trade, what do you do with the plates?'

"We toss them in a barrel, and when full, a company picks up the barrel of plates for recycling."

"Do you still have the barrel yet with plates from the 2018 blue Subaru Legacy?"

"Why, yes. You want me to look for them to verify your own records?"

"Yes, if not too much a hassle, Edward. My phone number is 303-619-4110. The plates are probably on top of the heap, I would think. Call me when you have had the time to find the plates."

***

Again, I leaned back, putting my feet up on the corner of my desk and did more brain-storming. If the plates Edward finds are the same as Dixie's, then she did change her name to Elsie Mae Dole. *Why? Trying to get lost? Need to find her. Clear shooting.*

I opened my computer to update Dixie's profile.

My phone rang. "Detective, there's an Edward Samples with Billings Subaru on the line."

"Thanks, Sally. Hello Edward."

"Yes, Detective. I rummaged through the barrel, and as you suggested, they were near the top. The plates are Colorado NRS409."

"Edward, the Elsie Mae Dole you know is the same woman I know by the name of Dixie Tallman. We need to locate her relative to the death of her ex-husband. If Elsie Mae contacts you for service or whatever, have her call me at 303-619-4110. It is critical that she contacts me."

"Detective, we have no phone number for her. She indicated that she would bring in the Beatle for service in two or three weeks. I did give you her address, didn't I."

"Yes, you did. Best I write her immediately. Thank you for your help, Edward."

"It's been my pleasure to help solve your mystery lady, Detective."

CHAPTER 24
ELSIE MAE DOLE

I checked out of my hotel and placed my luggage and valise in the trunk of my beautiful green Beatle. "How alluring you are Little Green Bug," I said out loud as I slipped behind the steering wheel. I chugged down Highway 310. I opened the window and drove with my arm resting on the door. "I'm free as a bird in flight! "I shouted to the world.

Nearing Bridger, I googled the address of 510 W. Sunny Side Avenue. In no time I was parked outside of Priscilla Brunings' home. What an appropriate street name for the attractive two-story house painted white with green shutters and trim. The lawn was manicured to perfection with four rose beds all in bloom. *How inviting. Tells me lady has pride.* I rang the doorbell.

"Hello, may I help you?" asked a lovely lady dressed in a yellow dress, her hair in a bun with a bright green scarf securing the hair with the ends of the scarf hanging to her shoulders.

"Margaret Finley of Spencers sent me to see you. I'm Elsie Mae Dole."

"I'm Priscilla. How wonderful for Margaret to have you come to see me. She is a great friend of our family. Do come in, please. May I offer you some coffee, tea, pop, water? You may be thirsty in driving from Billings."

"A glass of water would be refreshing."

"By all means, water it is. Come into the kitchen and have a seat. I'm curious why Margaret asked you to see me."

"Well, Priscilla, it's about the Shaker Peg Plaques your mother made for her."

"Oh, yes. My mother loved fashioning the plaques to meet the décor of any room in the house. Even a funny one to place in the basement to scare the mice, if any."

"Now that is going to an extreme in woodworking!"

"Yes, but my mother had a quirky sense of humor."

"Priscilla, I would like to buy the business. I do crafts and Margaret needs more plaques."

"Where would you set up shop? There is a considerable number of tools and material to box up. Do you have a home or apartment to use?"

"No, I don't have either. I'm living at the Quality Motel. I just arrived in your town. You're the first lovely resident of Bridger I came to see."

"Elsie Mae, I may have a solution for you. Come with me upstairs. The steps are a bit narrow due to the chair lift we installed for my mother. This hallway leads to a bedroom, living room, kitchen and a full bath. Everything is just like it was when she died of COVID. This is the second time I have been in these rooms since her death. Probably needs a thorough cleaning—dusting especially."

I checked all the rooms. "They are beautifully furnished. I love the antique writing desk."

"The shelves and the frame for the mirror were made by my late husband. He was a great handy man. He retired from 20 years as a real estate salesman. He bought houses as fixer-uppers and turned a great profit. He did all the work in changing the small bedroom or nursery into a kitchen for mother. She had ladies over from the church to chat. She was able to make refreshments for them. She had a bridge club twice a month."

"How charming. Really inviting rooms for living."

"Elsie Mae, since you need a place to live, I'll rent this to you if you approve. Now let's go to the basement and survey her plaque operation. If you wish to rent the up-stairs apartment the basement would be free for your business. You wouldn't need to move a single nail or brush."

"Priscilla, you drive a bargain that is hard to refuse."

"I have ample income to live on. To help you, I would ask $200 for the business and $250 per month for room and board.

"Priscilla, you are an angel in a gorgeous yellow dress. You have solved a huge problem of mine with the snap of a finger, so to speak. I gladly accept all the terms you stated."

"What is priceless would be your company, Elsie Mae. I have been very lonely since mother died, and then more so with my beloved husband's death after almost 30 years of marriage."

"I am so sorry for your losses. Do you have children, Priscilla?"

"No, I couldn't bring any from conception to birth. Had three miscarriages. How about you?"

"I'm single after seven years of marriage. My husband was a loving husband for about four years. Then drugs and booze destroyed him. I put up with him for three years, before I had to divorce him. I did so to save my life from the drunken punches I no longer wanted to endure. Restraining orders meant nothing to him."

"I am sorry you had to live through that life."

"Thank you. We both have had to suffer losses."

"You can move in right now if you like and cancel your motel room."

My laundry room is in the basement, so I come down here to see her working many times."

"I see that you have a chair lift for her to the basement."

"She hated stairs and it really helped her. Here are ten plaques in various stages of completion. You would have an excellent opportunity to get your feet wet, so to speak, to finish them."

I surveyed all the supplies that Ann used to make the plaques. "This is an ideal setup that your mother put in operation. I know I can do this. I noticed a kiln in the corner. Did she do ceramics also?"

"Yes. She made ceramics that Luellen Conley, manager of Joy of Living would suggest that would sell. She ordered raw ware from different companies. Let me show you the catalogs she used. You may wish considering this means of income after getting the plaque business underway."

"Good suggestion. You said room and board. That means all meals are prepared by you?"

"It certainly did! I love to cook and making food for one extra, would be no problem for me. Besides, I hate eating alone. Okay with that, Elsie Mae?"

"I'll be at your table with a fork and knife in my hands, ready to chow down."

"I love the way you said that. Do you need help bringing in your luggage?"

"All I have are two suitcases, and a small valise. Before I get them, you have no problem in using your mother's furniture and other furnishings? Is her clothing still in the closet?"

"Oh, my goodness, yes. I forgot all about them. I'll round up some boxes and empty the place. My mother and you must have the same sizes. I have overcome any sentimentality of her possessions, so check what you would like to wear of hers and I'll get rid of the rest."

"Priscilla, this is so overwhelming, I can't find the words to really express my gratitude. You have solved so many situations in one fell swoop, that I need to pinch myself to make certain I'm not imagining all this happening."

"Elsie Mae, you are God's gift to me to continue my mother's business and your companionship to remove the lonely hours I have had to endure for over two years."

We hugged and tears of happiness rolled down our cheeks. We broke into a roll of laughter that broke the tension.

CHAPTER 25
DETECTIVE MICHAEL

I booted up my computer to write Elsie Mae.

To: Dixie Tallman nee Elsie Mae Dole

From: Detective Michael Dorsey of Aurora Police Department

Date: 20 October 2022

Subject: Immediate contact to resolve death of Dan Austin

I have been attempting to maintain a profile of your flight and the reasons why you have tried to get yourself lost, apparently to your usual ways of living.

In talking to your former employer, Sam Stevens, I have a more solid story of your former relationship with your ex-husband, Dan Austin.

Visiting with your former landlady, Helen, she provided more evidence of your desire to travel within the United States and across the ocean.

We need to know what transpired precisely after Dan Austin, more or less, abducted you near Stevens Financial Services. We need to know what you did and what Dan did before he was found dead.

I finally tracked you down to living in Billings, and later to Bridger, and your change of name before you traded your Subaru for the Beatle. Edward helped me with the numbers from the Colorado plates removed from your Legacy.

You have two options to choose from: You can go to the Billings or Bridger police department and make a deposition.

Give them my letter for contact information. They will mail your statement to me.

The better procedure is to call me. See letterhead. I will record your statement and I would have the opportunity to ask questions on information that you may not have included.

The gun involved, a .22 caliber Smith and Weston, has been sent to our department from the Laramie Police Department who retrieved it from a box seat of the Albany Hotel. When the death of Dan Austin is resolved, you may obtain possession of the gun. However, you will need to have it registered in your name for it is presently under the name of Dan Austin. You do not wish to have what can be considered a stolen gun in your possession.

Please take action of this request upon the receipt of this letter.

CHAPTER 26
ELSIE MAE DOLE

After moving into the inviting rooms of Priscilla's home, I could not be happier. Everything seemed to work out beyond any expectations on my part.

I made great strides in the following two weeks of my accomplishments. I had finished the ten plaques that Ann had started. Driving to Billings, I delivered them to Spencer's. Margaret Finley was beyond jubilation when she unpacked my work.

"Elsie Mae, you did it! You came through with flying colors for me. And I have special orders for you to complete. Your work is as exquisite as Ann's. She would be pleased to know an angel answered her prayers. She had sent me a letter three days before her death of being so sorry not to be able to furnish me with more plaques."

"I tried to do my very best work."

"Here are the special orders. A fan of Betty Bop wants a plaque with her décor. I think there is a music box with her on it. A man wants a John Deere motif. You probably can find a small tractor in the toy store. A golfer wants a combination of Jack Nicholas and Tiger Woods. If you can find bobble heads of those two, that would be super with that décor. Ann brought most of her items from Hobby Lobby. While here in Billings, you may wish to see what is available."

"Thanks for the tips. I will stop at Hobby Lobby before going home."

"Elsie Mae, Ann would be so pleased to know an angel answered her prayers."

"Margaret, you're going to have me bawling, very shortly." I left with a $200 check--my first income!

Since, I was in Billings, I decided to have my Beatle serviced. I drove into Subaru Dealership. Edward was right there welcoming me as soon as I drove in.

"How did you know I was coming here, Edward. Are you gifted with clairvoyant abilities?"

"No, I saw your Beatle coming down the street from my window and turning into our lot. That simple."

"Okay. Well do you thing with my Darling Bug!"

"I'll drive it to the department immediately. Oh, by the way, Detective Michael Dorsey with the Aurora Police Department needs you to contact him immediately. He told me he would write a letter to your P. O. box. Here is the sticky note of the number he gave me."

"I haven't checked my postal box. Didn't expect any mail. I had it only as an address for you to trade cars and to get my driver's license."

"He shared with me that it was very important to contact him regarding the death of your husband."

"My ex-husband. We were divorced over three years."

"Oh, I didn't know that."

"How in the world did the detective know where I was living?"

"He tracked you down, apparently, to our dealership and your Colorado plates when we traded the Legacy for the Beatle. I did not know you were trying to avoid any contact with the police."

"Those damn car plates! Here I changed my name legally, trying to start a new life and those blankety blank plates destroyed everything to live my life without any hassles. I don't want to talk to any policeman. I want to start a new life—want to be left alone--now it's all over."

"I sorry, Elsie Mae. Sometimes life gives you lemons. In this case, you certainly don't want to make lemonade. We'll have your Bug ready in an hour. Our lounge has refreshments."

"Thanks, Edward. I have some catalogs to study to wile away the time."

***

When I left the dealership, I googled Hobby Lobby and soon found their parking lot. I couldn't believe how many different items they had on the racks for me to use in designing the décor for any situation. I bought what I thought would be helpful to go along with the supplies Ann had left.

As I drove back to Bridger, I dreaded the thought of a letter waiting for me in my mail box. I pulled the letter out and shoved it into my purse. I drove home and went directly to my living room. I held the letter, my hands literally shaking, making it difficult to even open it. I sat down and read the words with difficulty, not realizing I was crying. After reading the letter twice, I decided to write my story that I could read over the phone to the detective.

I moved to Ann's antique writing desk. There was her blank sheets of paper and envelopes. How convenient for me. But, now what do I say without implicating myself. Well, here goes.

I was leaving Stevens Financial Services on September 1. I had quit my job, asking Sam Stevens for my funds that he had held in escroll for me. I had a letter from the First State Bank to have a large sum of money in my possession. It was my intent to drive to my apartment, pack my suitcases, call for Uber to the Denver Airport to fly on to Dulles Airport and from there to Paris.

As I was walking to my car, my ex-husband, Dan Austin, grabbed me and roughly threw me into the back seat of his car. I knew he had been drinking alcohol or on cocaine, or both, and very angry. He jumped behind the steering wheel, and raced very fast down the street, weaving among cars. Suddenly, he pulled up to the curb while braking to a stop. He turned to look at me and apologized for manhandling me. He asked me if I had my gun ready to use because of carrying so much cash. Then he asked if he could check the gun. He complimented me on having a full magazine, a bullet in the chamber, and set on safety.

He put the gun to his head and said that I should rot in prison while trying to spend his money. He pulled the trigger. He slumped over on the steering wheel, his right arm falling down.

I was momentarily in shock. Then reality set in. He tried to make it look as if I had shot him with my gun. I panicked. I grabbed the gun from the front seat, shoved it in my purse, picked up my valise and scrambled out of the car. I ran down the sidewalk yelling at a lady to tell the driver of the bus to wait for me.

I realized that my white and yellow attire was like a flag. I went to Walmart and purchased some khaki-colored clothing. I asked a lady to drive me to my car. I drove to my apartment, packed some clothes, left a note to my landlord, Helen, and left for Laramie, Wyoming. While eating, I found a space in the box seat and dumped my gun in it, with the thought it would not be found for some time. The whole time, I was emotionally wrought and angry at Dan for taking his own life and to make it look as if I had done it.

I took my cellphone from my purse and googled for a map of the area. Should I drive to the West coast and fly to Hawaii or go to the East coast and fly to Paris. I decided going to Montana, find a small town and live there. I legally changed my name. The Legacy was traded for a Volkswagen. I thought that no one could find me living in Bridger, Montana. However, those

Colorado license plates gave me away when you called Edward Samples. He told me that I should contact you immediately. After I read your letter, I decided to call you.

I called the detective. His office forwarded my call to him.

"Detective Michael Dorsey. How may I help you?"

"This is Dixie Tallman, now legally, Elsie Mae Dole."

"Thank you, Miss Dole, for calling me. It is imperative that we know your side of the situation in resolving the death of Dan Austin."

"I have written out what you may desire to know. Can I read it to you?"

"Yes, you may. But give me a minute or two to have a recorder working to receive your message. The recorder is running. Please go ahead and start reading."

My hands were clammy and as I started to read, my voice went up to a soprano level.

"May I stop a minute or two to get a glass of water?"

"Oh yes. By all means. Take some deep breaths to relax yourself. We are not in any big hurry."

I drank a half glass of water, took two or three deep breaths, and began reading. That preparation certainly helped. I read through to the end.

"Miss Dole, that was a very thorough explanation. This will be a tremendous help in determining the results of this case on the death of Dan Austin. I have no questions to ask of you. The forensic team will be able to listen to what you read to me, and make a final decision. When I have received their report, I will write you the outcome. I do appreciate your cooperation. Good bye, Miss Dole."

"Good bye, Detective Dorsey."

I placed the phone in the cradle. I sat there in the chair, feeling like a rung-out dishrag. My hands were still clammy. *Glad it's over! What relief! How long to wait answer. Oh, well.* I walked rapidly to the basement and worked on my plaques. "It may help me to forget about this thorn in my flesh," I said out loud.

CHAPTER 27

TOBY

I was sitting with the rest of the Musketeers at our school lunch period.

"Can any of you help me to go to the place where we found the dead lady? Mike and the other polices could not find the shell casings in that tall grass."

Ken held up his hand. "I'll help. Why not use my dad's metal detector. He and I have used it to find all kinds of odd and neat metal objects at school playgrounds, camping sites, and even cemeteries."

"I can't help you. Sorry," said Slim.

"Neither can I," replied Rocky. "My mother said I should come right home after school to help her with shopping."

"That's okay. Ken and I will go after school."

***

I arrived at the place and drove on the short lane to the gate. Ken got out and opened it.

"Don't bother to close it, Ken. We'll be back in no time to go back out," I called out of my window.

We arrived at the large patch of grass between the two trees. Ken removed the metal detector from the trunk, turned it on, threw a nail on the ground to test the volume for the static sound the detector emits and walked into the patch of grass.

"Let's go in a circle around the place where the lady was, going a little wider each time around. We need to cover every square inch so we don't miss any spot," said Ken.

We moved no more than six feet when the monitor on the detector gave out a loud static noise that indicated something metal. Ken held the monitor in a stationary position, while I parted the tall grass. There was a shell from a .45 caliber gun.

"I'll pick up the shell with a nail and place it in a baggie I brought along," said Toby.

"That's an important find," said Ken. "Let's keep going in our circular pattern." Ken kept sweeping the ground as we made a wider circle.

Suddenly, his monitor gave out a loud static noise. "AH HA! Something else is in the grass. I'll hold it in the spot that is the loudest," said Ken.

"I'll pull the grass away carefully," said Toby. I fell to my knees. "There's the shot gun shell nestled in the grass.!" I picked it up with the nail and placed it carefully into the baggie, each casing in a corner. "That's two for two. Think there may be more to find?"

"Won't know until we keep sweeping the area," said Ken. He started walking forward and I followed right behind him. As we made a wider circle, the monitor gave out a loud static sound again.

"Hold the monitor on the spot, Ken." I parted the grass but it was an old can that was half rusting out. I picked it up and threw it out into the ground area. "Keep going, Ken. More surprises!"

As we made a wider circle, the monitor starting beeping again. "Another find!" shouted Toby. As I parted the tall grass, I saw another shot gun casing. "This has been here sometime from some hunter. The casing is full of dirt. Let's leave it."

"Let's continue, who knows what more is here," said Ken. He continued sweeping again. We were around fifteen feet from the center, being the place of the body. The monitor sounded off again with loud emitting sounds. "Something big!" exclaimed Ken.

"I'll move the wet grass away," said Toby as he bent over to do so. "Ah shucks, just another old can. Let's just leave it. I don't believe we will find anything more that Mike and the forensic team can use."

We walked back to the car. Ken placed the metal detector in the trunk. "Let's take these casings to Mike. I hope they will help solve their case," said Toby.

***

We arrived at the police station. "Hi Sally," said Toby.

"Well, if it isn't the rookie detective!" replied Sally.

"Ah, stop with the teasing, Sally. Is Mike in his office?'

"Yes, he just arrived shortly before you did."

"Ken, this is Sally who runs this entire precinct with razor sharp efficiency," teased Toby

"Touché! Toby," said Sally, "Pleased to meet you Ken."

"Pleased to meet you, Sally," replied Ken

"How about stopping all these formalities and go to Mike's office with our important findings," said Toby

***

Toby placed the baggie on Mike's desk.

"What is this?" asked Mike.

"These are the casings of the revolver and shot gun we found in the tall grass," replied Toby.

"You're kidding me, Toby. How did you find them?" as Mike carefully removed the casings with his pen and placed them in a small plastic dish.

"We used Ken's father's metal detector to find these easily in that tall grass," said Toby.

"Toby, you and Ken were certainly in the right place at a time when we needed hard evidence. Hope there are fingerprints on these casings," said Mike.

"We hope the casings will help you also. We both agree that your department needs to invest in a metal detector," said Toby.

"Okay Toby. I get the picture. You were able to accomplish what our team couldn't do."

"Something like that, Mike. I need to get Ken home. So long, Mike."

"Certainly, a pleasure to meet you, Ken. Thank your dad for the use of the metal detector."

CHAPTER 28
TOBY AND FAMILY

The family sat down for dinner after arriving home from church.

After dinner was over and everyone was finishing dessert and a glass of wine, Toby asked, "Hey Mike, did you ever have any results from the names and pictures of the Porsche at 1413 Cherry Street that the Musketeers obtained for you?"

"Oh goodness yes, Toby. We had some hard evidence when we were able to know the real names of Jerry and Judith Mathias and their butler, Carl Batson. All three were the main bosses of a drug cartel operating in Aurora."

"We had developed an ongoing profile of Carl Batson who seemed to do all the traveling. He seemed to shop every Thursday. Since none of the other detectives seemed to get anywhere with him, I though I'd give it a shot. We already had a search warrant to place a tracking bug on his car so we could follow him easily."

"Get on with what you did!" exclaimed Toby.

"I backed out of our driveway, and waited for Carl to do his shopping. Sure enough, it was Thursday when he left the house. I followed at a safe distance. He went to a wholesale company in the industrial park. I parked and watched with my binoculars. They are 20X power so I could read the names on the three boxes an employee carried out to his SUV. A case of Del Monte cocktail fruit, and a case of peas and green beans. My thought was, wow, that is a lot of food for three people."

"Ya, I'd get tired of eating green beans and peas every day," said Toby.

"I followed him to a King Super Store. He parked and went into the store. I was driving in as he left his car, so I parked close by. Before I could get out of my car, a black Ford pickup went to the back of the SUV, opened the door, threw those three boxes into the bed, and took off. I had copied down the license plate. I radioed to squad cars in the area, to stop the truck, arrest the men for theft, and save the boxes of food as evidence."

"Yes, did they catch the crooks?" asked Lucille.

"They not only apprehended the two, but when the boxes were opened at the precinct, they were packed full with marijuana, cocaine, and fentanyl."

"That warehouse must not be what everyone believes it to be," said Henry.

"You are so right, Henry, but nothing will be done until we get the ring-leaders, who might be Jerry and Judith Mathias. We need hard evidence to arrest them."

"What about, Carl? Did you see him in the store?" asked Toby.

"Well, I went into the store, found a shopping cart and looked up and down the aisles for him. I threw some bread, milk, and butter into my basket. I found him in the aisle for beverages and soft drink. As he was coming out of the aisle, I rammed my cart into his as if by accident. I apologized for being clumsy. He said, "No problem." He was wearing a cap with an unusual but beautiful bird on the front.

I asked, "What kind of a bird is that?" I pointed at his cap.

He took it off and looked at it. "That's a tropical bird called a Toucan."

"Never heard of that species. Can I look at it more closely?"

"Sure can," he said. He handed me the cap. I had already taken a "bug" from my pocket and held it in my closed hand. Our Captain had already had a search warrant signed by Judge Delbert Knight in order to plant it on the cap. Then I saw that the top of the patch was loose.

"Since you're beside the root beer, can you hand me two bottles, please?"

As he bent over to reach the bottles, I quickly slipped the "bug" behind the bird patch. He placed the two bottles in my cart and I gave him his cap.

"Thanks. Do you wear that cap a lot?" I asked.

"Every day from morning to night. It's my favorite. Well, I do take it off to shower and when sleeping."

We both chuckled.

"You were certainly flirting with danger," said Greta.

"You need to take a risk sometimes and fly by the seat of your britches," said Michael.

"Did the 'bug' bring you any evidence?" asked Toby.

"Did it ever. Since he had the cap on all day, we recorded huge **amounts** of damaging evidence when around Jerry and Judith. By their conversation, we realized the three were the head of the drug cartel in this area."

"I reckon' you arrested the three ring leaders?" asked Toby.

"Yes. We had a court order signed by a judge to search the house. A SWAT team of 10 and 5 policeman surrounded the house. The Mathias and Burton didn't resist and surrendered without incident when they saw all those guns pointed at them."

"Was there any good stuff on the computers," asked Toby.

"The amount of stored information and the current orders that were coming in from drug dealers were enormous. With the names and addresses available, we arrested forty individuals."

"Wow! That many?" said Toby.

"This was one cartel unit. There are more that need to be weeded out. How many, who knows," said Michael.

"How about the warehouse. That place must be full of drugs," said Toby.

"The same team that was at the Mathias house, surrounded the warehouse. The four employees had AR- 15's and started to give battle with the SWAT team. But six SWAT men came in behind the four and wiped them out. The warehouse had 89 boxes full of drugs. They were loaded in a truck and taken to our storage area at the police headquarters."

"And the boxes were real ones?" asked Lucille.

"Yes, the real boxes of fruit and vegetables were dumped in boxes, barrels, and piled on the floor. Then filled with drug orders and resealed. Fooled many people."

"What happened to all that good food?" asked Toby.

"We notified an organization that has Soup Kitchen scattered throughout Aurora. The canned goods were put to excellent use in feeding a lot of homeless people."

"So, the Musketeers had a big hand in helping you. Can we be awarded with the Porches?" asked Toby.

"Ah ha! You should be so lucky!" said Michael. "The Porches and Carl's SUV along with all the household furnishings will be sold at an auction."

"Who gets all that money? Is there a reward paid to me?" asked Toby.

"Toby, you're funny. It goes into the city's general fund but earmarked to help with the budget for the Police Department," replied Michael.

"Well, all is well that ends well," said Greta.

"That pretty much sums it all up," said Michael.

CHAPTER 29
DETECTIVE MICHAEL

The report of the forensic lab was on my desk. I read it with great interest

1. There was a partial finger print on the .45 Caliber casing. It was enough of the index finger of either the left or right hand to obtain a reading.
2. There was enough of fingerprints of the thumb and forefinger of the left or right hand on the shot gun shell's metal band to make a strong identification.
3. The prints were placed in machine for an ID match.
4. The partial print on the .45 casing belong to Johnny Saunders, last known address was 1948 Golden Street, Denver, Colorado 80206
5. Prints on shot gun casing belong to Gerald Schuster, last known address was 992 Jane Drive, Cherry Creek, Colorado, 80206

I walked the report to Captain Rayburn's office. "We have a sound report of the guns used in the death of Mary Jane Little." I gave him the report and waited for him to read it.

"That is hard evidence, don't you think? Can we pull together a SWAT team, surround these two houses and find out if we have the right murderers? "asked Detective Michael.

"Yes, Detective. This case does warrant special attention now. I'll have this, we'll call it the 'Big Little Operation,' ready to launch in two hours. You 're in charge."

***

I went back to my office. Opening my computer, I did preliminary searches on Johnny Saunders and Gerald Schuster. Both had prior arrests for vagrancy, speeding tickets, disorderly conduct with knife fights at Sam's Bar and Grill. To have gone overboard on committing murder would be a surprising addition to their rap sheet.

I joined the SWAT team, along with two other detectives who worked on the case with me, two policeman and one policewoman. We donned our protective gear.

When I approached the house on Grace Street, the shades were all pulled down. This helped the team to surround the house on the back and two sides without detection.

There were two cars, one parked on the driveway and the other on the street. This car had a smashed rear fender and large dents of both doors on the driver's side.

I rang the doorbell. A man opened the door who had a couple days of beard growth, wearing pants and a T-shirt, and bare-footed.

"Good afternoon, Mr. Saunders."

"That's me, What the hell do you want, cop?"

"I was on my daily patrol. Are you aware that someone side-swiped your car parked in the street?"

"The hell you say. Let me get something on my feet."

He came out on the porch with two younger men, probably in their mid-twenties, dressed in jeans and T-shirts, dirty and greasy appearance.

The three joined me as we strolled to look at the damages. "When the hell did that happen?" asked Mr. Saunders.

"I'm sorry, Johnny. I hit another car last night coming home. I suppose I had four too many beers," said one of the lads.

"Juan, you son-of-a-bitch, you. Now you tell me!" He threw a sucker-punch at Juan, who fell down, cracking his head on the pavement.

I grabbed Johnny to restrain him when he was about to kick Juan in the head. I pulled his left hand behind his back, snapped the handcuff on his wrist and pulled the right hand behind him and snapped the cuffs. Johnny was fuming and fussing so fiercely that I don't believe he was aware of being handcuffed.

The other young man helped Juan to his feet. "Thanks, Duffy. Johnny, I was going to tell you and pay to have the car fixed. Now you can go to hell!"

I gave a signal and the SWAT team came running and surrounding us. "Johnny, you are being arrested for the murder of Mary Jane Little." Two policemen cuffed Juan and Duffy. "I don't know if these two lads are part of the murder, but we will sort all this out at the precinct headquarters."

I started to give the three their Miranda rights, when Johnny blurted out, "I'm not taking this rap alone. Gerry was a part of the accidental death of her!"

"You mean Gerald Schuster?" I asked.

"Yeah. That son-of-a-bitch is guilty as hell!" shouted Johnny.

"For your own satisfaction, we are going to Gerald's house now. Detective Pete, you and Annalee can give them their rights and book them at headquarters."

***

Everyone left for their cars. I led the team to 992 Jane Drive. Everyone pulled into a parking lot a half block away. We moved stealthily to one side of the house. Six of the SWAT team jumped the fence to go to the other side the house. They didn't know a German Shepheard was in his dog house. When the dog heard the noise, he came out barking fiercely. One of the SWAT members had the presence of mind to grab a sack of donuts from his pack, and threw them at the dog. He stopped barking and begin chomping the treat. However, when all were devoured, he started barking again. But the six men had cleared the fence and were huddled against the side of the house.

Someone in the house came to the back door! "Shut up, King! Get your butt into the house. Your barking is goin to have the neighbors riled up and the cops called on us!"

I was able to get the last three out of the house easily and hand cuffed. What ploy can I use this time. I walked back to the parking lot and drove my car beside the Cadillac parked in the street.

I had a valve stem cap in my pocket and screwed the valve stem out. The tire went flat quickly.

This house had a two step to a small porch area. I pushed the doorbell. A man in an expensive suit and tie, with highly polished shoes opened the door. He was holding his dog by the collar that was growling loudly. "Shut up, King!" I noticed him twisting the collar in a form of choke hold.

"Hi. I'm Mike Dorsey with the police department. I was on my regular neighborhood patrol and noticed you have a flat tire. I see that you are dressed nicely and, on your way somewhere. Can I change the tire for you? Is your spare, okay?"

He slipped out the door quickly so the dog couldn't follow him. "This is right neighborly of you. Didn't know you cops would help us citizens and taxpayers."

"Well, we do. You may not hear of what we do. That's an attractive shirt with a monogram on the pocket. GS. Does that stand for a 'Great Sport'?"

He laughed. "No, it's my initials—Gerald Schuster. But everyone calls me Gerry."

"Please to meet you, Gerry." I held out my hand and we shook. "Anyone else in the house beside King?"

"No, I live alone. No hassle that way with anyone else."

I gave the signal. Everyone came running and surrounded us with guns aimed.

"What the hell is going on. You bastard, you. You tricked me. You ain't a good cop!"

"Detective Mitchell. Handcuff our friend, Gerry. Gerald Schuster, you are being arrested on the charges of murder of Mary Jane Little. You have the right to remain silent..."

Gerald interrupted me. "I am not taking this rap alone. Johnny and his two nephews were in the accidental shooting of her."

"Gerry, those three are already in jail waiting for you to join them."

"You cops are all alike! Can't trust a frickin' one!"

"Can Johnny and you be trusted to tell us the truth and nothing but the truth as to how Miss Little was murdered?" All I received was a menacing glare of eyes that spelled hatred.

"Detective Nicholas, give him his rights, book him, and have him join his friends but different cells. Don't want them to collaborate on any topics. Bob, you have a way with dogs, try to get King on your side and take him to the rescue dog pound. I'm sure they can find a new owner. Detective Jim and Stan, we have a warrant to search Gerald's house for evidence—guns, ammo, drugs or anything else. Then, we'll go to back to Johnny Saunders's house for the same purposes. Perhaps we can find some connection of his two nephews to the murder. Rest of the SWAT team, great work. Thanks for the back up."

Detective Stan placed a hand on Michael's shoulder. "You're good, really good! Arrested them outside their houses. No guns had to be fired. Slick as a whistle!"

"That's the beauty of trying to use brains rather than brawn. Sometimes it works. I was a bit apprehensive. I didn't know if one or more would pull a gun. We didn't do a body search."

***

"As your Police Commissioner, I am pleased to report today, that the arrest of the individuals responsible for the death of Mary Jane Little, have been apprehended, awaiting arraignment and trial. Detective Michael Dorsey, along with the help of his brother-in-law, and his friends, found the body east of Aurora in a stretch of undeveloped land. A team of your police department, under the direction of Detective Michael Dorsey, made the arrest of the persons involved, without any shots fired. He was able to gain a degree of trust and had them outside in the open and charged with the crime involved. When we have completed the arraignment and deposition of these persons, we can release their names and other pertinent information. Thank you for your attendance.

CHAPTER 30
DETECTIVE MICHAEL

I booted up my computer. I'm certain that Miss Dole will appreciate this letter.

Date: November 1.
To: Miss Elsie Mae Dole
From: Detective Michael Dorsey

Subject: Resolve of Dan Austin's death

You have undoubtedly been waiting for the results of our Forensic Team.

With the evidence the team found in and about the car Dan Austin was driving the day of his death, along with your detailed explanation of the events following your abduction, the Forensic Team has concluded that you are in no way involved with his death.

Evidence was beyond any doubt that Dan Austin committed suicide with his own gun he asked you to give him to check. Traces of gun powder was present on the plastic glove he was wearing, on his wrist above the glove, and on the passenger seat cover when the gun fell out of his hand.

As mentioned in previous letter, if you wish to claim the .22 caliber gun, please inform our department of your intentions.

CHAPTER 31
HERBERT AND DENISE PENCE

I crunched the newspaper into a ball and threw it on the floor. "Denise, did you read the article in the newspaper about the hot-shot detective by the name of Michael Dorsey? He must have such an ego; his wife can scoop it up with a spatula."

"No dear, I haven't read any thing about this detective you seem to loath."

"I know for a fact that the Little woman was a big snitch. She had been ratting to the police for some time. She finally met her reward.

"Herb, that is a strange conclusion--death as a reward.".

"I call 'em as I see 'em."

"What do you plan to do about it? Isn't that you're biggest challenge?"

"The police commissioner didn't give names, but that dick arrested Johnny, Juan, Duffy, and Gerald. Earlier, Jerry and his wife, Judith, and my pal Carl were also arrested plus a bunch of drug dealers. Police rubbed out four guys I knew at the warehouse."

"I'm sure some brilliant mind will come up with some type of retaliation. Right, Sweetheart?"

"I'm angry from losing so many friends. Someone will meet the challenge and get revenge that will smack him right between his eye balls."

"That does sound inspiring, to say the least, Dear Hubby."

CHAPTER 32
TOBY

"**K**en, I need to go to Walmart after school and buy two spiral notebooks for Mrs. Tompkins's History class. I need the extra credit by outlining the history lessons."

"Toby, I'm in her class too, but a different hour than you. I need some notebooks too."

"Let's go there right after school and then I'll take you home."

"Sounds like a plan, Toby. I do appreciate the extra gas you use to haul my butt home."

"Glad to do it for you my martial black-belted friend. Meet you at the flagpole."

***

I drove into the Walmart parking lot. "There's my sister's car. Must have been buying groceries." I parked several cars from her's. "Let's go talk to her. She is sitting in her car. Either she just got here, or ready to leave."

I rapped on the window with my key. She didn't move. I tried the door. It was locked. "Ken, try the doors on the passenger side."

"Both doors are locked."

"Strange!" I pulled out my cellphone and punched in Michael's number.

"Detective Michael Dorsey, how may I help you?"

"Mike, Mike, this is Toby. Lucille is sitting in her car unconscious! Doors are locked! Could she have suffered a stroke or heart-attack? Do you have her car keys on your ring of keys? Somebody else has already called 911. I heard him ask for an ambulance and EMT's. Can you leave right away to the Walmart parking lot on Sable? Should the EMT's break a window if they get here before you or the police? What do you want me to do?"

"Toby, slow down so I can answer you. I'll radio squad cars in the vicinity to arrive there in short order. I'll tell them the problem. They have tools and the skill to open the doors. Yes, if the EMT's get there before me or the police, break a rear window. I'm out to my car now."

True to Michael's word, two police cars came wheeling into the lot. Ken and I, as well as two other men, waved frantically to the drivers to where we were. One policeman ran to Lucille's car and slid a thin bar down the window and in no time had the door open. The other policeman was stringing tape around the perimeter of Lucille's car.

The policeman reached in and placed his fingers on her carotid area. He shook his head. "I'm sorry to say the lady has no pulse." He called the corner. He pulled his mic to his mouth. "Detective Michael, do you copy?"

"Yes, I hear you."

"Please get here as quickly as possible."

"I'm already in my car and five blocks away now."

Ken and I moved to the side of the car and watched. I looked at my sister. *Dead! Terrible! I'm sad. Mike sad. Mom and dad sad. Will miss her terribly. Why? She had good health. God, grant her life in your paradise.*

I watched people coming and going from shopping and begin to stand along the tape before them. People whose cars were within the perimeter of the tape asked if they could leave. I was close enough to hear their request and the policeman's question. "Did you see or hear anything when getting out of your car to shop?" None had any helpful information.

Mike pulled into the lot and came running, ducking under the tape. An officer said, "I'm sorry, Mike, to inform you that we found your wife had no pulse. An EMT also verified the same diagnosis."

Mike went to look at his wife. I went to Mike. We did a man hug. Our eyes were wet from forming tears. "Are you going to call Mom and Dad, or do you want me to tell them the sad news?"

"I'll do it Toby." He walked a few feet away from me and I watched him talk to my parents.

The coroner arrived and made his inspection and recorded information on a form he had on a clipboard. "You EMT's can remove the lady."

The EMT's lifted Lucille from behind the steering wheel. "Is that blood on the car seat?" asked one EMT.

The coroner examined the seat closely. "It appears to be blood. Move the body inside the ambulance so we can do more of an examination."

One EMT opened her coat. The other EMT opened the rest of her clothes. "Look! There are two bullet wounds, one apparently through the heart, and the other is higher and went through a lung. This is murder, isn't it? We can certainly rule out a stroke or heart attack."

The coroner examined the bullet holes, lifting up the body to check the exit wounds.

"Yes, this is murder. I'll need to revise my report and finish it after the autopsy is completed."

After Michael had finished talking to his in-laws, he went to the ambulance, having watched them move his wife as he was talking.

"Detective Michael, your wife was murdered. Two obvious gun shot wounds. Better get the forensic team here immediately to Walmart on Sable to make a thorough examination."

Michael pulled out his cellphone and called into his precinct. "Have the forensic team come to 630 Sable, Walmart, immediately. My wife appears to have been murdered."

All the cars within the taped perimeter had been allowed to leave. Michael and the two policemen removed the tape and made the perimeter smaller. As he was doing this, he surveyed the people who had moved up to the replaced tape. Talking to the two policemen, "I'm getting the strange sensation with the hair standing up on the nape of my neck that the person who has a vendetta against me is watching us. Who could it be? My wife didn't have an enemy in the world. So, it maybe something I've done, and wanted to get revenge by killing Lucille."

Toby heard what his brother-in-law had said. "Ken, I'll put my cellphone on video, slide it in the pocket on my arm. Then we'll walk along the tape looking at the pavement as if looking for something as evidence. They won't know I'm taking their pictures."

So, Toby and Ken walked inside the perimeter of the tape, with Ken picking up stones and bits of debris.

After completing the video, Toby said, "Ken, let's take pictures of the cars parked now and video the license plates. Mike might be able to acquire IDs on them by getting names and addresses."

Toby walked behind the cars in five rows, ignoring the cars that were coming into the parking lot. Having completed taking the pictures, they returned to stand near the ambulance. The coroner had completed his examination and left. The forensic team arrived.

Again, Toby watched the team taking pictures, dusting for fingerprints, studying the holes in the upholstery, and extracting the lead slugs from the car cushions.

Michael watched as the ambulance left for the city morgue. Toby, filled with sorrow, watched Michael shake his head in disbelief, following the ambulance disappearing into the distance. *Who did this? Why? Need to find the person. Where to start?*

Toby approached Michael and placed a hand on his shoulder. "Mike, what can I say. There will be some sad days ahead for you and for us. Do we move Lucille's car or will Walmart complain if we leave it overnight?"

"It's best I drive it to our precinct headquarters in the event the forensic team wants to do more examination. You drive my car. Ken can drive your car. You take Ken home. I'll drive to your folk's place. I just can't go to my house tonight."

"Sounds like a plan, Mike. Check your cellphone for some pictures that may help you. I heard what you said about someone in the crowd might be the murderer. So, I tried to do what you didn't have time to do yourself."

"Thanks, Toby. It may be that you were in the right place at the right time once again.

CHAPTER 33
TOBY AND FAMILY

The family gathered at the Rodriquez's family home for dinner after all had attended church.

Toby volunteered to give the blessing.

"Father God, we gather together with your blessings. We look to You for mental support as we spend time in sorrow. We are thankful for you means of Grace. It will help us to get past the sorrow and move to a happiness for Lucille's resting with You in paradise. Your love for each of us will help us more through the days leading up to her funeral and the following days. Give Mike a special cup of courage in the coming days. We are thankful for the love and sympathies we are receiving from relatives and friends. Bless this food we are about to partake. In Jesus name we pray. Amen"

Greta touched Toby's hand. "Thank you for the meaningful prayer for the family. It is so fittingly given along with the pastor's prayer for us this morning. Mike, you can use our guest room as long as you wish. We understand not wanting to live in your own home now."

After the dishes of food had been passed around, Mike looked at Toby.

"I can't believe what I viewed on my cellphone. The pictures of all the people were sharp as a tack. The pictures of the cars were spot on. I'll have the pictures downloaded by our forensic computer team. I'll have my secretary list all the plates in numeric order.

We'll call the DMV and ask for names and addresses a few each day. Then somehow, we will need to eliminate names as we gather more evidence. What that will be will cause all the detectives some critical brain storming."

"Mike, I have a strong feeling that you'll get a break and will be able to arrest the person or persons."

"Toby, you are certainly more optimistic than me."

"Mike, there's a lady that seems to live at Walmart sitting down with a shopping cart filled with her stuff. Who is she? Is she permitted to hang around the store?"

"Oh, that would be Tillie. I met her dozens of times when I had the beat on the streets of Aurora. I would chat with her and give her money to buy food. I even took her to restaurants and bought a good hot meal for her several times. She likes the Walmart area because people are kind to her. In the summer time, she takes care of people's dogs while they shop. The cars get too hot for pets. The off-duty policeman who are on security watch her belongings when she uses the bathroom facilities. Introduce yourself the next time you go to the store. Her speaking of English has a lot to be desired. So don't be too critical of her as you visit with her."

The meal continued with more pleasant topics. Then the family enjoyed watching two football games, a movie from Netflix while eating popcorn, apples, pretzels and drinking root beer.

CHAPTER 34

ELSIE MAE

I picked up my mail, if any, once a week. Detective Michael's letter was there.

I ripped open the envelope expecting bad news. There was a bench nearby. Sitting down quickly, I scanned the letter, then read it slowly.

I gave out a sigh of all sighs. Dan's death was of his own choice. I am cleared of everything. WHOOPEE DO! In a spurt of thrilling action, I threw the letter into the air. Other postal patrons looked at me as if I had lost my marbles. I didn't care! My thoughts were free of many nagging sensations I had mentally bottled-up in my head since I saw Dan pull the trigger and tried to make me the murderer.

I sat on the bench, reflecting on all that I had done to try to disappear in the town of Bridger. Had I known what I know now from the detective's letter, I would not have had to leave Aurora. Oh, well, here I am with a different name, a differed type of living, and a few other new changes. But I am happier now than I could ever realize.

Picking up the letter, I headed for my beautiful green Bug waiting just for me. I am free to make plans to travel where ever I please! What a refreshing feeling! Paris, here I come!

CHAPTER 35
DETECTIVE MICHAEL

On Monday morning, I gave my cellphone to our computer video forensic examiner. She down loaded the video of the crowd of people standing along the security tape. She made prints for us to use. I enlarged the images of the faces and the four of us detectives studied them carefully.

Mike pointed out a situation. "Why did this one man who was standing on the right side of the crowd, duck down behind everyone and come up to the left side. The audio is weak. But. do you hear the man say, 'What are you boys searching for?' Then, Toby's voice is distinct, with an answer, 'Evidence.' "That portion was replayed several times.

"Mike, I believe that's what is being said. Why is this man especially interested in what the boys are doing? You have a brilliant brother-in-law to have taken the initiative to video the crowd of Looky-Loo's," said Detective Tom.

"Yes, Toby and his pal, Ken, also videoed all the parked cars. My secretary has listed the plate numbers numerically and is calling to obtain the names and addresses of the car owners. That may help down the road."

"That's awesome for Toby to realize that the murderer's car could be in the parking lot.

We may need to have him with us as a rookie civilian detective, Mike," said Detective Harry.

"Yes, he is smart. Straight A's in high school. Graduates this year and plans to go to University of Colorado. He videoed 22 cars. Far too many to call on each person once we know the owners. Somehow, we will need to whittle the list down to the car the murderer is driving."

CHAPTER 36
TOBY

The janitor at Michell High has the routine of moving the lunch room tables back and forth to clean under them. It was on a Wednesday and he had moved the table that Toby and his friends occupied only four feet from the table of the Demos.

Toby and his friends were sharing the highlights of their football game and the enjoyment of basketball starting soon.

However, Toby was listening to the Demos conversation. He found himself concentrating on the directions of the leader over top of the talking of his friends.

"Demos, we are having a rumble tonight at Washington park at 7:30. We have information from a snitch that the Ambass are having a picnic with some of their bitches. Bring your heat and enough ammo. We need to reduce their number. We'll gather at the entrance to the park at 7:15 and tighten up our car pool to four each."

Toby continued to eat his lunch and join in the conversation. *Need to call Mike. SWAT team to stop it. Could be bloody!*

Toby left the lunchroom and headed for the outside door. He strolled to the flagpole, looking up to watch the flag slipping back and forth in the wind. He waited for Mike to answer his cellphone.

"Detective Michael Dorsey, how...."

Toby butted in. "Mike, this is Toby. I overheard a bit ago that the Demolition gang plans to ambush the Ambassadors at Washington Park at 7:30. The Ambass are having a picnic with their wives and girlfriends. You may need a lot of backups. The Demos at Mitchell High are 10 in number, but they are part of a larger gang."

"Thanks, Toby, for the information. We'll take over from here."

CHAPTER 37
DETECTIVE MICHAEL AND OTHERS

I went immediately to the captain's office. Rapping on his door, he invited me in.

Relaying all the information that Toby had given me to the captain, he stood up quickly.

"Damn those gangs! They have had several rumbles in the past as you well recall. Now we're having another one. Troubling situation to prevent deaths and bloodshed. I'll get on it right away and organize a SWAT team, with all of you detectives and 12 policemen all in combat protective gear. I'll get the word out immediately to everyone to meet in the parking lot at 6 p.m. for more details of meeting the Demos."

***

Everyone gathered around the captain.

"The SWAT team will ride in a school bus. We can't use any marked vehicles or we will give ourselves away. Ride four to your own vehicles. I see that you all are in protective gear already. There are two policemen in civilian clothes at the park already. They will determine the spot where the Ambassadors are having their picnic. The information will be sent to me. The roads at the park are one way. We will drive in and park along the curb. Between other people's cars if necessary. There is a parking lot we may need to use."

"Captain, can we hunker down beside our cars so we can spring into action quickly?" asked Detective Michael.

"By all means. When the Demos arrive, they may park outside of the park and walk in. Or they may drive in and leave their cars in the middle of the road with plans to surround the Demos. We don't know what they will do, but I will talk to you on your radios. Be certain they are working. I believe they will choose to drive in. Michael will drive in the wrong direction. This will cause the lead car to stop and the rest also. Rush up to the cars, pointing your AR-15's against the window. Yell at them to drop all weapons on the floorboard and get out with their hands clasped above their head. If anyone of the Ambassadors as much as points a gun, use the necessary force to stop the threat. Hand cuff two persons to each other and take them to the school bus. Gather all the guns left in their cars. Select an SUV to collect the cache. I'll be at the entrance of the park and let everyone know when the gang starts into the park."

Unknown to the Captain, the Demos had four of their gang on watch also. When the watchman at the entrance to the park recognized Johnny DeMarco's' car of the Ambassadors, he immediately called Juan Michell, leader of the Demos. The Demos scrambled for their cars, leaving all their picnic items on the tables. The plain clothes policeman seeing this take place, immediately called the captain. "The Demos had a lookout, evidently, and are in their cars and speeding away."

The captain grabbed his mic, "Abort, abort! The Demos had a spotter, and have already left the park. Let the Ambassadors drive through, so, Detective Michael, don't block the road. "

The Ambassadors had a watchman who was sitting in his car near the picnic area with a pair of binoculars and was not aware of the police team having entered the park, hiding. When he witnessed the Demos leave hastily, he called Johnny Demarco on his cellphone and informed him that the Demos must had been alerted and had left in a hurry.

The captain watched as the Ambassadors left the park. He picked up his mic, "Team, it appears everyone was watching everyone but us, so the rumble didn't happen today, but will one day soon, I fear. Let's go back to headquarters and call it a night. Thanks everybody. Proud as hell of you all."

CHAPTER 38
DETECTIVE MICHAEL

Mike called Toby early before he went to school.

"Toby, two members of the Ambassadors were shot and killed last night in a drive-by shooting. They were both nineteen years old based on divers' licenses. It may have been the Demolition gang, but not certain. We haven't much to go on yet. Were shot with a 9mm. Someone on the street told us they saw a black Chrysler that was, apparently, well restored. The last year for that make was the early 1960's. We have an all-point bulletin out now. You might check the parking lot at your high school for the possibility that it could belong to one of the students. Probably not likely, but a shot in the dark."

"Okay, Mike, I'll try to get some information somehow, if possible."

***

The school janitor had the tables where Toby sat over 10 feet from the Demolitions' table. He could hear the talking that sounded jubilant, but couldn't make out any words being spoken. He knew if he tried to eat his lunch at their table, the conversation would certainly be changed.

***

"Hey guys, I need to use the john. If I'm not back before you leave for class, let's meet at the flagpole right after school. My brother-in-law, Michael, could use the Musketeers to do some sleuthing for him."

CHAPTER 39

TOBY

As I entered the boys' toilet, four students were leaving. Opening the door to use the stool, I entered and locked the door. I no more than sat on the throne, when two students came in to the toilet laughing their heads off. In a minute or two, I smelled marijuana being used. *School should install vents. Good grief! Breathing that stuff like smoking it.*

"Are we alone in here?" asked one student.

"I'll check if I see any shoes, "said the other student.

Toby quickly raised his legs way up.

"Nope. No one in the shit stalls. Only a back pack someone left. We can talk freely."

Toby pulled out his recorder very slowly from his backpack he had placed on the floor. He pushed down the "ON" lever. It made a click sound. He held his breath hoping they did not hear it.

"Good. We're alone. We really wiped out two of the Ambass assholes last night. Two clean shots! They never knew what hit them. We need to reduce their frickin" numbers even more, when possible," said the other student.

"Yeah, we sure need to. Trouble is, the Ambass creeps will try to kill some of us now in revenge."

"We certainly need to be on our guard."

Toby could not recognize the voices. He knew he had to remain absolutely still. He grabbed his leg trousers to help hold up his legs. There was a small space between the door and the rest of the metal support. He was able to recognize the face of Anthony Trujillo. *Who's the other guy?*

The other student said, "I need to use the john for a bigger job. Damn those snotty kids! They lock the door, then crawl out from under the door so no one can use the john. I'll try the other stall. Good, it's open."

"Okay, Paul. I'll finish this hit and go on to class. See you later, bro," said Anthony.

Paul? Paul? Who the heck is Paul? thought Toby.

Whoever was Paul, had finished, flushed the stool, washed his hands and left.

Toby was greatly relieved. He lowered his legs, finished his chores, flushed the toilet, washed his hands, then peeked out the door. He only saw students moving up and down the hallway to their classes. He joined them.

***

Toby met the other Musketeers at the flag pole after school.

"Michael told me that two of the Ambassadors were wasted last night. They suspect the Demolition to have made the hit. Michael states that someone saw a 1960 or '61 Chrysler. It was really a work of restoration. Really sharp. Have you seen that kind of car in our parking lot? Mike reasoned that it would be unlikely a student would have money to buy and restore an old Chrysler."

"No, I haven't seen a car of that description in our school parking lot," said Ken.

"I know for certain that the Demos did the hit job. I was in the toilet sitting on the stool when two Demos came in. I had to raise my legs when they checked if alone. They freely talked about 'we' having killed two of the Ambassadors. I was able to record their conversation. I need to get the tape to Michael today yet."

"That was a risky move on your part, Toby," ventured Slim.

"I took the risk. They were really excited and spoke in loud voices that helped to prevent them from hearing me. Anthony called the other student by the name of Paul. Who is that?"

"Oh, yes, that would be Paul Reasoner, a new student that started around two weeks ago, added Slim. "I tried to talk to him but he brushed me off."

"Great going, Slim. I'll give the names to Michael along with the tape recorder. He can get the addresses from the school files. I'm going to the police station now. Your buses to take you home have already left, so come with me and then I'll make the circuit to take you home."

CHAPTER 40
DETECTIVE MICHAEL

Michael phoned Toby that same evening.
"Sorry I wasn't in when you left the information on my desk. I listened to the recording of the two Demos. Really revealing. At least we know that the Demolition gang did the killing. We will follow up on the two gang members speaking on the tape. How did you record them?"

"Well, Mike, when I was in the toilet using the stool, these two Demos came in the john. When they checked to see if alone by looking for shoes, I had already lifted my legs way up. I was able to pull my recorder from my backpack very silently and turn it on. They spoke very freely and loud, also, which helped to cover up any sounds I may have made. I could ID Anthony Trujillo, and Slim was able to help me ID Paul Reasoner."

"That was risky, Toby. But you took the opportunity to help us. I will call the school and get the addresses of the boys' parents tomorrow. May have two good leads to start solving the murders."

"When the two used 'we', that may not implicate the two Demos, but 'we' referring to the whole Demo street gang. But as you stated, you definitely know the Demolition did the hit."

"That is really an astute observation, Toby. We'll bring them in for some deep questioning.

Thanks again, Toby, for the good leads to follow up. I'll bring back your recorder tomorrow."

"No big hurry. Did you ever find the Chrysler?" asked Toby.

"Yes, we did. It was owned and driven by Alfonso Rodriquez, no relative of your dad. He claims he was alone that night and insisted he was not involved in the drive by shooting. He did have a solid alibi that we checked out thoroughly. However, he is a member of the Demolitions. I saw the car. It was professionally restored and really a classic. I saw what appeared to be two bullet holes in one fender."

"Must be a wealthy guy. Wonder how he makes his living-- Drugs? Prostitution ring?"

"Good point Toby. We may need to do more digging about Alfonso. See you tomorrow."

CHAPTER 41
DETECTIVES MICHAEL, TOM, AND BOB

"Tom, Bob," said Michael, "I called the principal at Mitchell, and explained why we needed the addresses and names of the parents of the two students. He gladly obliged me and we have the first step in arresting these potential assassins. You two take Paul Reasoner. I suggest you make the call around five o'clock when Paul is home."

***

Tom and Bob approached the attractive green two-story house. They observed that the neighbor's homes and landscaping was in good taste. Tom pressed the doorbell button.

Mrs. Reasoner answered the door. "Hello."

"I'm Detective Tom Dillard with the Aurora Police Department. This is Detective Bob Dolsing. Is Paul home, Mrs. Reasoner," asked Tom.

"Yes, he is. Do come in, Detectives. He's up in his room playing his guitar or watching Netflix"

"You do know that your son is with a street gang called the Demolitions. We need to question him about a murder of two rival gang members," said Bob.

"He's what? He never told me anything about a street gang."

"We're sorry to tell you this. Most members don't tell their parents," said Tom.

"I'll get him." She went up the stair steps partway and hollered, "Paul, get down here now!"

Paul came into the living room cautiously. "These detectives are with the Aurora Police Department. What did you do that causes them to come here to see you?"

"Nothing, Ma. I don't know why they are here. I'm no mind reader," retorted Paul.

"Don't get smart! Why are you with some street gang called the Dem or Demmo, or whatever the name is?" asked Paul's mother.

"Who says I am?" questioned Paul.

"We do, Paul. We have on solid authority that you are a member of the Demolitions. We are here to determine if you are the person who pulled the trigger and killed two Ambassadors two nights ago. Anthony Trujillo tells quite a story," said Tom.

"I don't know what you are talking about," replied Paul.

"We know you joined the Demos recently, but Anthony Trujillo has been a member for some time. We listen to the conversation of you two that was recorded in the toilet at your high school." Tom pulled out his note book and read, "We really wiped out two of the Ambass last night. Two clean shots. They never knew what hit them." He slid the notebook into his pocket. "Now, the 'we' is either you or Anthony? We have a warrant to arrest you for the murder of the two Ambassadors." He pulled out a pair of handcuffs and cuffed Paul. Tom patted him down.

Tom looked Paul squarely in his eyes and read him his rights.

"I didn't shoot those guys. I don't even own a gun!" exclaimed Paul.

"That excuse doesn't fly. You could have used a gun given to you," said Tom.

"Neither Tony or I killed those two Ambassadors," said Paul.

"Well, someone in the Demolition gang did. That we now know for certain. If the 'we' in the recording of your conversation refers to the Demolitions, then can you give us the name or names?" asked Bob.

"I'm no snitch," snarled Paul.

"I figured that would be your answer. Mrs. Reasoner, we are taking Paul to our headquarters for further questioning," said Tom. His cellphone beeped. He opened his text screen. "Just arrested Anthony Trujillo and taking him to headquarters. Wouldn't 'talk."

"Sorry, Mrs. Reasoner, to have your son arrested in the solving of this murder case. We will inform you as we proceed. You can visit him at your leisure," said Tom.

CHAPTER 42
CAPTAIN RAYBURN

Detectives Tom and Bob arrived at their precinct with Paul. They went through the proceedings of booking him and placing in a cell. Michael had already arrived with Anthony and had completed the process.

Tom and Bob stopped at Michael's office. "I see you typing up your report. We better get in gear and do the same."

The detectives took their completed reports to the captain's office. He immediately read them.

"Those street gangs are a pain in the ass. Almost had a rumble at the park. Tight lips, those gang SOBs. It's getting late. Let them stew in jail overnight. We will question them tomorrow. Maybe more likely to talk. At least we know that the Demolition gang are responsible for the death of the two Ambassadors. We may need to arrest more of those that we know already have rap sheets. Good work getting these two Demos arrested. That brother-in-law of yours, Mike, is certainly in the right spot at the right time to get the recording of the conversation. Never would have thought a toilet would be the right place to get useful evidence. See you tomorrow. I need to burn some midnight oil. Have a ton of work to do. Good night, detectives."

"I'm staying late, too, Captain. I'm taking Robert and Roger to the Fitness Room and do an hour of exercise. Plan to join the boys."

CHAPTER 43
ALFONSO RODRIQUEZ

"Hi, I'm Alfonso Rodriquez," as he entered the Aurora Police Department around five o'clock. "I need to see Captain Rayburn now. It is very important that I see him. Hope he's in. Very urgent!"

"Yes, that's possible. The captain is still here. You need to go through security screening first. Remove everything in your pockets and place it in this bowl. Your jacket and belt in this plastic container."

Alphonso emptied his pockets. He reached to his back and remove his gun and placed it in the bowl.

The security guard did a double take when he saw the gun.

"It's not loaded. Would you take it to Captain Rayburn and place it on his desk? He will want it I know for sure."

***

Alfonso was escorted to the captain's office and given permission to enter.

"This is a great surprise," said the captain. "The security guard brought me this gun and that you needed to see me immediately. Have a seat Mr. Rodriquez."

"Captain, that is the 9mm gun I used to kill the two Demolition gang members."

"That is quite an admission of your actions."

"Yes, it is. But let me explain. I'll even volunteer to take a lie detection test. I killed the two young men in self-defense. If you want to record what I am about to tell you, that is fine with me."

The captain picked up his phone and called the forensic lab. "Please bring a recorder to my office now to record a deposition."

The machine arrived and was set to record.

"Okay, Mr. Rodriquez. tell me how this 9mm was used in self-defense."

"I was driving on Prince Street, which is in a rundown neighborhood looking for houses that need painting. As I was driving slowly, a Chevy passed me and then immediately pulled directly in front of me. I braked quickly and was able to stop with my bumper against the passenger door. I knew immediately that I was about to be ambushed for I recognized the passenger as a member of the Ambassadors. I figured they wanted to kill me in order to steal my classic Chrysler."

"Yes, I saw a picture of your Classic that Detective Michael Dorsey had taken when it was found behind Frank's Bar and Grill. Great restoration work."

"Yes, it is a beauty. Well, I jumped out, pull my gun, cocked it, and ran to the back of my car. The driver must have done the same. I fell to the pavement to watch his footsteps from under my car as to where he was. He knew I was behind my car. I jumped up quickly when he was beside my car door and shot him in the chest area. He went down immediately. I looked to see what the other Ambassador was doing. He was just sliding out of the driver's door. I bent down to the pavement again to watch his footsteps. He started around their car, but stopped and reversed himself when he saw his buddy on the pavement. He walked slowly around his car and was coming up alongside of mine. He stopped by the passenger door. Again, I jumped up as an element of surprise and shot him right below his chin. He fired at me but I had already jumped back behind my car. His bullet hit my fender and came out the back end of it. I bent down to see where his feet were. I saw him fall to his knees and then on his face. I jumped up and saw no one. I threw my gun on the seat and scrambled into my car. Again, I didn't see anybody. I backed up and drove rather fast to get out of the area. That's about it. Captain. I hated to kill them. But it was them or me situation."

"That is quite a rendition of self-defense. So, you now have two bullet holes to fix on your classic? Why are you volunteering all this information to me?"

"Well, you have two young Demos in your jail now taking the rap for the two murders that I did. Anthony's mother called me and shared the information that her son and Paul Reasoner had been jailed. I can not live with my own conscience to have them spend their life in prison if proven guilty even as accomplice because they are members of our Demolition group. I'm 85, Captain, and have terminal cancer. The doctor has given me about a year to live. Let me spend the rest of my life in prison for the murders, and release the two young men. Is that a satisfactory trade?"

"Mr. Rodriquez, sorry to hear about your shorten life issue. In all my years on the force, I have never had a case of this kind.

"As for my shortened life span, I can live with it. Have to. I hope you will consider the release of Paul and Anthony and put me in the cell instead."

"That can be arranged. But if this is self-defense, the situation changes considerably."

"Well, I'll let you work out the problem with my attorney, Jason Ridley. He should be arriving here soon, for I asked him to come to this police station."

Alfonso looked at his watch. "Excuse me, Captain. I need to call the Demolition leader, Reggie Salvo. They are holding a meeting now. Need to give them the information of my surrendering to you and the release of the boys. Also, to get the community service project as a priority."

"That's okay. Go right ahead."

"Thanks for allowing me to contact my group. Where were we?"

"I read the report of Detective Dorsey. When your classic was discovered parked behind Frank's Bar and Grill, he learned that you had been there when the ambush, as you stated, took place. You had an airtight alibi."

"I suppose that's due to loyal close friends." I smiled. "Something else you may not know about the Demolition and Ambassador gangs. I am making inroads to have a safety zone of around two blocks between us across Aurora so the rumbles will cease and these hit jobs will stop. I have had the leaders of the two gangs at a peace treaty at Franks'. I paid for the meals and the beers. There are three pool tables and we all had a very cordial afternoon of friendly activity. So, I am trying to have the gangs do community service."

"I've haven't heard any thing about this community service. Why the secret?"

"Well, the Demolition men just started last fall. I drive up and down streets where houses are not kept up. I stop and visit with the owners. If it is a rental, I look up the owner.

I ask them if they will furnish the paint, we will paint the house. I bought a van that carries the ladders and all the stuff needed. Members have trucks. We clean up all the trash around the house and haul it away. When the weather gets warm again, we will continue. Last fall we were able to paint six houses. That is why I was driving on Prince Street looking for houses that need a face lift. I find owners that can't afford the paint, so I have been spending out of my pocket."

"Mr. Rodriquez, this is really a great revelation!"

"I guess it about not tooting our own horn."

"Well, if you don't have any objection, I'm going to give you some publicity. Now, you have a bad rap in the community, especially among the police force."

"Not a necessity for publicity, Captain. I am trying to get the Ambassadors to do some community service, also. They are hesitant to start."

I turned off the recorder.

***

Detective Dorsey knocked on the captain's door.

"Come in Mike," said Captain Rayburn. "You already know Mr. Rodriquez."

"Yes, I do. Hello to you, Alfonso. Certainly, different seeing you here talking to the captain. This is Jason Ridley, Alfonso's lawyer."

Captain Rayburn came from behind his desk. They shook hands. "Have a seat."

As the captain was walking to his chair, he said, "Mr. Rodriquez has already shared a blow-by-blow story as to how he had to kill the two Ambassadors as a matter of self-defense. We have recorded his deposition which you can hear. Usually, a client has his lawyer present for it. I believe his story in defending his own life. The two he killed were trying to ambush him in order to steal his car. However, he got the drop on both of the Demolition members to save his own life. The report and pictures taken at the murder scene showed the two Ambassadors on the pavement with their guns still in their hands. Their car was parked across the street as you described. He wants us to place him in jail and have the two young men released. Detective Dorsey will move you two to one of the interview rooms. You can listen to the recording. Work out the legal details for his arraignment. Tomorrow you can meet with the District Attorney, Marsha Blackburn, who will be back in town from working on another case. Detective Dorsey, take the necessary steps to release Paul and Anthony and take them home to their parents. I'm certain they will be happy to see them.

CHAPTER 44
REGGIE SALVO

"Let's bring this meeting of the Demos to order," shouted Reggie over the loud jabbering of the members. Tubby, why in the hell are you waving your arm in the air as if batting down bugs?"

Tubby looked back and wilted a little from all the snickering. "I heard that Alfonso with his classy car was stopped and questioned by the police as to his whereabouts after the hit on the two Ambassadors."

"Yeah, Tubby, we know about his being found at Frank's Bar and Grill and grilled by a detective. Remember our code of silences. If you should waste any of our rival gang in a shootout, you tell no one. If any of us are arrested and threatened in questioning, there is no way in hell that you can reveal any name. The police have no leads that I know of at this time. We need to keep it that way. Understand?" asked Reggie.

"But won't someone in our Demos be in danger now from the vengeance of the Ambass?" asked Clyde.

"That is very possible," answered Reggie.

"Where are Anthony and our new member, Paul," asked Clyde.

"Does anyone know about any of those missing tonight's mix, especially Alfonso?" asked Reggie. "No dope on anyone?" His cellphone beeped. "Excuse me, Bros. Could be important." He went out of the room.

When Reggie came back into the room, he yelled for order. "That was Alfonso. He is at the police station now and has admitted that he shot the two Ambassadors in self-defense who ambushed him and tried to steal his Chrysler. He got the drop on both. Anthony and Paul are in prison for the murders or accomplice to the murder. Something about their voices on a recording that implicated them as having killed the two Ambassadors. Alfonso is working out the details with his lawyer and the district attorney to be booked and arraigned. He will go to prison and Anthony and Paul freed."

The silence in the room was unusual for several moments.

"Around two weeks ago, Alfonso called for a peace treaty at Franks Bar and Grill. Pete, Dan and I were there. The three leaders of the Ambassadors were present. After a great meal and some beers, the six of us played several games of pool. I have to admit, everyone had a great time. Alfonso had us agree to a two-block safety zone stretching across Aurora. He wants us to stay in our zone. No rumbles. No more deaths. Are there any objections to this new arrangement?" asked Reggie.

"Aren't we taking some of the excitement out of our gangs' existence?" asked Clyde.

"Do we want to vote on this new deal?" asked Dan.

"Fair enough. Any discussion? All those opposed to the new arrangements, raise your hand," said Reggie.

"Let's have a secret paper vote," said Pete.

"Fair enough," said Reggie. "Secretary Randy, hand out some paper ballots."

The vote was taken and counted. "We have 13 'yes' votes and 'one' no." responded Randy.

"It appears you approve the new rules for the peace treaty. I know our wives will be happier than us. We have too many widows in our gang," replied Reggie. "At our next meeting we will work on the program we started last fall of painting houses and sprucing up neighborhoods. Alfonso told me that he has informed Captain Rayburn what we have already done. We have been given a bad rap by the entire police force. And the community at large. We need to change or we will all be facing some prison time, sooner or later. Agree?" asked Reggie.

"Hearing no objections (Pause)--we are done. See you at next week's meeting."

CHAPTER 45
TOBY

"Mom, I must be growing. Look at my shirt sleeves and my ankles as to how short my clothes are?"

"Oh dear. Toby. Yes, you are sprouting. You're way taller than I. Let's go shop after you come home from school."

***

"Mom, there is Tillie the Street Lady that Mike told us about. Let's go introduce our selves."

They approached Tillie sitting on the steps to the entrance of Walmart. "Hello, Tillie," said Toby. "I'm Detective Michael Dorsey's brother-in-law and this is my mother, Greta. I'm Toby."

"My goodness! Please meets you both. Toby, youse a good-lookin' lad. And Greta, nice to meets you. Mike sure good friend for long time. Help me more than once, he did."

"Yes, Tillie," said Greta, "Mike has told us how you like this area. People are good to you and helping people in the hot summer days with their pet dogs. Can we bring you some hot coffee? Rather chilly today."

"That be goods of you."

"We will see you later, Tillie. Need to buy some clothes for my growing son," said Greta.

***

"Toby, pick out three pairs of jeans and a good pair of slacks, four shirts, a sweater, and a sport coat."

After Toby picked up his sizes, he went to the changing room to put on the slacks and the sport coat. "How do you like this combination?" asked Toby.

"Son, you have good tastes. However, your dad is going to make a double take when he sees the monthly credit card statement. How about shoes?"

"They are very tight, Mom."

"I'll pay for these items. Go change to your school clothes, then we'll go to the shoe department."

After the purchase of two pairs of shoes, Toby said, "Gosh, we have been here over an hour shopping for my stuff. Is there anything you need from the lady's department?"

"No, I'm fine. Let's pay for these shoes and then go to the restaurant and get coffee and a sandwich for Tillie."

***

"Tillie, wake up! We have your coffee for you," said Toby.

"She is really sleeping," said Greta. "I'll shake her shoulders." She placed her hands on both shoulders and shook her. Greta stepped back. "That's strange."

"Mom, there's a trickle of blood running down the steps. We better call an ambulance and get some EMT's here!" He pulled out his cellphone from his sleeve pocket and punched 911. "Please send an ambulance and some EMTs to Walmart on Sable. We have a lady that doesn't respond."

Toby placed his fingers on her wrist. Mom, I don't feel a pulse. Maybe I don't know the right place to check her pulse." He punched in Mike's number.

"Detective Michael Dorsey, how may I…"

"Mike, this is Toby. We introduced ourselves to Tillie before going in to shop. When we came out an hour later, she doesn't respond. There is some blood on the steps where she is sitting."

"Okay, Toby. I'll get a squad car there right away."

***

The ambulance and two EMTs arrived in short order, followed by a police car. They all ran to Tillie. One EMT placed his finger on her carotid artery. The other EMT had an oxygen mask ready to slip over her head.

"The lady is dead, Officer. No pulse," said the EMT.

"Do you see the blood that is trickling down the steps?" asked Toby.

"Oh, wow! She must have been hemorrhaging," said the EMT as he placed the oxygen equipment away.

The police officer grabbed his mic. "Detective Dorsey, do you copy?"

"Yes, I do."

"This woman is dead. Perhaps from bleeding out. Better call the coroner to come to Walmart on Sable," said the policeman.

"I copy that. I'll call him. I am five minutes away."

People out of curiosity started gathering too close to Tillie and the others. The policeman went to his car and returned with a roll of tape. As he fastened it to poles and other structures, he urged the people to back up.

Mike arrived, braked quickly, and came running to the scene. He looked at Tillie. "In the span of one hour you talk to her and then she's dead! How can that be? My good friend, Tillie, that I have known for at least ten years."

The coroner arrived. He started his examination. "That blood on the steps concerns me. Would you EMT's place her on your gurney and move her into the ambulance. I need a more thorough examination."

Tillie's two coats were removed. They pulled off two sweaters, two pair of slacks were cut off along with underwear items. The coroner gasped. "There are two-gun shots wounds. One through the heart and the other higher through her lungs." He called for Mike to come to the ambulance. "Mike, this lady was murdered. Two shots, one to the heart and the other to the lung. Check the cement steps where she was sitting. See if the slugs are still imbedded in the cement."

Mike went to the steps. There were the two smashed bullets. He rolled them in a plastic bag and returned to the ambulance. Then he surveyed all the people standing behind the tape.

"Horrible! Simply horrible, Toby, I'm getting the same vibes as when my wife was murdered here. The person who shot Tillie is in that group of people. The murderer can't resist watching what is taking place. He wishes to gain a rush from the killing." Toby and the policeman looked at the Lookie Loos.

Toby pulled out his cellphone, set it on video and placed it in the pocket on his sport jacket. He walked along the tape looking at the pavement as if looking for evidence. He walked slowly and steadily to capture good images of the people. He completed the square. He realized more people were stopping out of curiosity, so, he made a second walk beside the tape.

When he got back to Mike, he said, "I have a video of everyone. Do you want the cars videoed as well?"

"No, Toby." He approached the policeman. "Would you copy down all the license plate numbers of the cars that are now parked. The one who murdered Tillie is in that group of people. I'm certain of that. Toby videoed all the cars when my wife was murdered here. If the same car appears again on another list, we may have a person of interest to follow up."

Mike went to Tillie's shopping cart of her possessions. He carefully lifted each item, examining each and checking the pockets. Toby came up to Mike. "What are you looking for?"

"Toby, I'm hoping she has some letters or some notes that may help find her next of kin. You can help me search for anything helpful."

After twenty minutes of searching many items of clothing, nothing was found that would be of help. "I don't even know her last name," said Mike." Isn't that terrible?"

Mike called his precinct headquarters and asked to speak with the captain.

"Hello Mike, what can I do for you?"

Mike gave the captain the full story of what had taken place. "Do we need to have the Forensic Team to complete any more examinations?"

"No, under the circumstances you outlined, I don't believe it is necessary for the forensic team to be there. Your report and that of the coroner will suffice in this murder case. Any suspects, Detective?"

"No, unfortunately not. But I have a good hunch that I will follow up on," said Mike.

"I just knew you would, Detective. Get the SOB that killed an innocent woman like Tillie."

"Thanks. If the same car is on the two lists of the two murders, we may have a possible lead."

Mike helped the policeman remove the tape as he watched the people going to their cars. *I know one of you is the murderer! Darn certain!*

CHAPTER 46
HERBERT AND DENISE PENCE

"**D**enise, did I miss the story in the newspaper or didn't the paper print anything about the death of Mr. Dorsey, the detective's wife?"

"I didn't read any story, Herb. I did see her obituary, however."

"That is very strange why that murder didn't make the news. All the other murders have a story."

"Can't help you any, Dear."

"I need to find out who the young man is that I believe was taking pictures of the people at the murder scene at Walmart."

"Why? Were you there?"

"Um-m, yeah. I went to Walmart to buy some work gloves. My old one had holes in them."

"Well, I do recall that Mrs. Dorsey had a brother listed in her obit. His name was Toby Rodriquez, I believe. The dead woman's husband is Detective Dorsey."

"Oh yes. That would be Detective Dorsey's brother-in-law. Why was he at the Walmart when Mrs. Dorsey was murdered.?"

"I can't help you. Perhaps he was there buying something at the store the same time you were there and found his sister murdered. Poor lad! Must have been terrible for him to have that happen to him. Even worse as the detective's wife. How awful. Hope they find the murderer."

"Don't be so morbid, Denise. Life and death are part of our existence."

CHAPTER 47
TOBY AND FAMILY

Another Sunday dinner was held after church at Detective Michael's home.

After prayer, the dishes of food were passed around. Toby looked at Mike with great intensity.

"Mike, are you suffering inwardly more than I can sense from your outward actions and conversations?" asked Toby.

"Toby, I loved your sister very deeply. I miss her terribly. But from another of my viewpoints, life must continue. I'm at that point that my life must mean more than it was before. That's what you probably are trying to express about my actions and words I choose to use."

"Okay, Mike. I understand. Now what do we do about Tillie. That murder makes no sense at all."

"I agree. However, it is interesting to know that the same man you videoed at Tillie's murder was also in the video you made of your sister. Is that just a coincidence? I really don't think so. The car is registered to a Herbert Pence, the address I don't remember, but have it in my profile of him."

"That is more than a coincidence, don't you think?" asked Henry.

"Yes, but not enough of evidence to make any arrest just to question him," answered Mike.

"Sooner or later this Pence guy will make a big mistake, a big one. Then you may get him dead to rights," added Toby.

"I like your thinking, Toby," said Mike.

CHAPTER 48
TOBY

"Toby, your dad and I will be gone for two days and nights. I want you to stay with Mike for that length of time. I have asked Mike and he said it would be super to stay with him," said Greta.

"Okay, Mom I'll go there after the basketball game. I'll pack a few clothes for school and my tooth brush."

***

As Toby was pulling up to the curb at Mike's house, a car was parked in front with the driver's door open. *That's strange.* He pulled out his cellphone from his sleeve coat pocket and took a picture of the car. He was about to shut off his car lights and exit the car, when a man came running down from Mike's porch to the car. Toby still had the cellphone in his hand, so he snapped a picture of the man looking at him before he jumped into the car and sped off down the street.

Toby went to the front door and rang the doorbell.

"Come in, Toby. Was expecting you. Just watching Law and Order."

"Mike, as I drove up, a man ran to his car, jumped in and tore down the street. Did he ring your doorbell?"

"No, you're the only one to ring it."

"What's this paper fasten to your door?"

Mike pulled it loose, closed and locked the door after Toby entered. He turned on the hall light. He read the note. "Well, who the hell is following my career?" He gave the note to Toby who read it aloud. YOU ARE SUCH A DUMB DETECTIVE; YOU COULDN'T FIND YOUR WAY OUT OF A CARDBOARD BOX."

"I wonder who the hell put that on my door?" asked Mike

"Perhaps this will help you." Toby opened his cellphone to the photos, and gave it to Mike.

"Toby, I can't believe you had the presence of mind to take pictures.You are certainly in the right place at the right time once again." Mike enlarged the photo of the man. "For Pete's Sake, that is Herbert Pence and the same car license plates that belongs to him. Why that son-of-a-bitch! Wish I had positive proof that he's the murderer of my wife and of Tillie."

"That note certainly appears to be baiting you to do something drastic," replied Toby.

"I'm going to pay him a visit and try to flush him out."

CHAPTER 49
DETECTIVE MICHAEL

The next day, Mike went to the residence of Herbert Pence. He rang the doorbell, then knocked on the door loudly three times.

Herbert opened the door. "Well, surprise, surprise! How are you Detective Dorsey? Is this a social call? Do come in. This is my wife, Denise."

"Please to meet you Mrs. Pence," said Mike.

"Have a seat. What can I do for you as a member of our distinguished law enforcement?" asked Herbert.

"Well, for starters, look at this note that was fastened to my door last night," said Mike.

Herb took the paper from Mike and looked at it. "Who wrote this?"

"Apparently, you did. Don't you recognize your own printing?"

"You are accusing me of doing this?"

"Yes, I definitely am. Here's proof." He gave Herb copies of the two pictures Toby had taken.

Herbert looked at Mike rather sheepishly. "Where did you get these pictures? Do you have a camera on a pole by your house?"

"It doesn't matter how the pictures were obtained. Why are you baiting a member of the law? You know that can be a misdemeanor and subject to an arrest right now."

"Oh, Detective, can't you take a joke?"

"No, I cannot. Not now or at any other time. Especially, this type of a prejudicial taunt of a police officer."

"Are you going to arrest me now, Detective?"

"Not at this moment—perhaps later." Mike turned and left the house, leaving Herbert considerably bewildered.

CHAPTER 50
HERBERT PENCE

"**D**enise. You left the room after I introduced you to the detective."

"Yes, I decided for the two of you to have a conversation without my being present."

"Well, did you hear what was said?"

"Yes, I did, Dear. I was in our computer room and heard every word. Why in the world did you put that note on his door?"

"Well, the house was dark and didn't realize I would be caught. Was trying to have some fun with the detective. It must have been the car that parked right behind mine. He had to have taken pictures of me and the car."

"You need to be more careful, Sweetheart. You are going to get into big trouble."

"Do you think he knows who killed his wife and the poor street woman sitting at Walmart?

"Could be. What poor woman are you talking about? I didn't read anything about that. Why are you so concerned?"

"Just wondering. That's all. But who the hell took the pictures of me running from the house to my car?"

"You better watch your step, Dearie. I don't want to visit you in any jail."

"I'm going to drive by the detective's house and see if that car that came up behind me is still there. I need to get the plate number and go to DMV to get positive ID of the owner. See you later."

CHAPTER 51
DETECTIVE MICHAEL

Mike took the photos of the group of people standing along the tape to the captain. He had circled the picture of Herbert Pence. He laid the photos and the note plus the picture ofrunning to his car.

The captain looked at the display. What does all this mean, Detective?"

"Well, Captain, the man circled was at my wife's murder and at Tillie's. He was caught running from my house after fastening this note to my door. Does that not cause Herbert Pence to be a person of interest for further questioning?"

"Certainly, looks suspicious, Detective. This appears to be circumstantial evidence. I can't get a warrant to arrest him. You will need hard evidence to have a judge write one for us."

"I did stop at his house for a visit about this note. He tried to deny doing it, but when I showed him these pictures by his car, he tried to change his behavior and story of having some fun with me—a big joke."

"What did he do or say?"

"Well, I mentioned that he was using prejudicial taunting of an officer of the law and could be arrested on miscellaneous charges."

"What was his reaction to that ?"

"I left the house so he could stew about what I might do later."

"Mike, you are a rascal; a clever one at that!"

CHAPTER 52
TOBY

I t was the morning of the last day of staying with Mike. I entered my car to drive to school. As I started to pull away from the curb, I looked in my rear-view mirror for any traffic. I saw a car parked down the street a half block away, thinking nothing about it. I entered the lane of traffic. When I came to the stop sign of our street, I noticed that the park car had come up behind me. *Hum-m. That car looks familiar. Wonder why?*

When I turned right to a two-way street, the car followed me. Again, I didn't give any thought to that regular event.

The speed limit was 35 MPH and as I drove steadily, making some quick glances in my rear-view mirror, I wondered why he was tail gating me.

Suddenly, I saw the car accelerating to pass me. As the car came along side of mine, I happen to make a quick glance out my window. I froze as I saw the man pointing a gun at me. Instinctively, I hit the brakes as the bullet shattered the window beside me. I had to brake even more as the car whipped in front of me and the car ahead of him to avoid oncoming traffic.

I grabbed my cellphone from my sleeve pocket and was able to get two pictures of the backend of the car before he pulled out to pass the car ahead of him and speeding far over the speed limit.

I pulled over to the shoulder and turned off the motor. *That's too close to death.* I was literally shaking. I leaned back breathing deeply. Pieces of glass had covered my lap, the floor and dash board. Having the cellphone in my hand yet, I tried to get my fingers to punch in Mike's number. I knew he was still at home.

"Hello, this is Michael Dorsey."

"Mike, that guy that I photographed when putting the note on your door just shot at me while driving!"

"What? Really! Oh No! Are you okay, Toby! I can't believe Pence would do that! Did you get hit?"

"Yes, I think I'm okay. Just shaking in my boots, literally! Can you come and rescue me? I'm in a pile of shattered glass. Can't be more that a mile from your house on Allen Road."

"I'm leaving now, on the way to my car. Hang tight!"

I leaned back with my head on the resting cushion trying to move my heart from my throat to its regular place. A picture flashed in my mind if I had not hit the brake on a reflex. Since I had been driving at 35 MPH, the car certainly would have careened off into the ditch, perhaps rolled over, or crossed over to the oncoming traffic and cause a serious accident. I spoke a prayer out loud. "Thank you, Lord, for the protection from the evil one. May You soften his hard heart so he too can rest with You one day in Your Paradise. Amen."

I continued sitting with my eyes closed, breathing more regularly now with the shock slowly ebbing away. I didn't even hear Mike park behind me and until he said. "Are you okay Toby?"

He opened my door. Pieces of glass fell out into the road. "Give me your cellphone, Toby, so I can take pictures of the broken window and the glass all over your clothes. I don't see any cuts on your face, thank goodness. You do have a couple nicks on your hands, though."

"Is that groove on the dashboard from a bullet?"

"Why I believe it is. He must have shot twice. The first shot destroyed your window and out through the passenger window that is shattered also. Why don't you get out of the car, so, I can snap a picture of that groove. Hey, the slug embedded itself into the car post. We are in luck!" Mike pulled a baggie from his breast coat pocket. Using a pen, he was able to wiggle the slug loose and into the container. "I know we have some evidence we need now to arrest that dangerous character."

"I have pictures of his car, too. He had to whip in front of me due to oncoming traffic. I had the time to take two shots before he raced around the car ahead of him."

"Toby, that's tremendous thinking under the circumstances of being shot at. I'll have these pictures downloaded by our computer forensic examiner. With prints made, I'll take them to the captain. This may convince him that we have the hard evidence to get a warrant to check Pence's house after arresting him and his wife. I get the feeling that his wife knows nothing about his killing streak. Maybe she does. We'll sort that out."

"Mike, I'm going to be late to school now."

"Toby, you just went through a big shock to your body. Are you sure you are ready for school?"

"Yes, I think I can handle it. I feel calm now."

Let me take you to school then. I'll go in and talk to your principal. I'll pick you up at 4:30. Is that about the right time?"

"Yes, Mike. Do appreciate what you are doing for me. I think I was in the wrong place at the wrong time on this attempted murder."

"Oh, Toby. The Lord was watching out for you. I will go to our precinct headquarters, pick up another detective to drive your car back for more examination if necessary."

"Okay, Mike. Sounds like a plan. I have already thanked the Lord for sparing my life."

CHAPTER 53
DETECTIVE MICHAEL

Mike returned to his office after dropping off Toby at his high school and visiting briefly with the principal.

He had just dropped off the cellphone to the forensic examiner's office when he was told to pick up his phone for a call from the morgue.

"Hello, this is Detective Michael."

"Detective, when we removed the two pairs of stockings from Tillie, we found an envelope between the pairs. It gives the information you may need. Her name is Tillie Norton, and the address of a nephew—Jacob Bentley, 4349 East Quebec Street, Denver, CO 81004."

"Good! That is most helpful. I'll contact this Jacob so he can claim the body for burial when it's released by the morgue."

***

Mike went into the captain's office. He showed the pictures he had taken of Toby and his car and told him what had transpired on the attempted murder.

"Detective, write up the report in detail and bring it to me. I will need documentation to get the warrant signed by the judge to get that character arrested and to search his house for more evidence."

"I'm on it, Captain."

CHAPTER 54
HERBERT PENCE

"Damnit! Damnit! I missed that peep squeak! He must have seen the gun pointing at him and hit the brakes slowing him just enough to miss. All hell is going to break loose now!"

I continued driving down the road with my anger seething through me, finally slowing down to the speed limit. Good thing I did, for I met a patrol car.

Driving home, I moved Denise's car to the street and parked mine in the garage. *That might help!* I continued to sit in my car thinking what the hell I needed to do immediately. I wondered how long it might be before that pesky detective makes his move. I thought I had everything thought out, so, I had a perfect crime. No detective could solve the case. Now I made a serious mistake. That darn note started to unravel my plans. That was too cocky of me! But how the hell was I to know that the kid took pictures of me when parking behind my car. Now I missed killing him. Crap and Shine Nola!

I finally went into the house and sat in my chair. Denise came out from our computer room. "I didn't hear you come in. What's wrong? You look as if you saw a ghost!"

"Sweetheart, sit down. I need to make a confession. The person who killed the detective's wife and the street lady at Walmart was me. I tried to rub out that young kid this morning who has taken all the pictures at the murder scene and of me at the detective's house. However, I missed because he hit his brakes and caused me to miss. I'm going to be arrested for the attempted murder of the kid and possibly of the other two women. You may be arrested too, although you are innocent."

"Herb, you big dummy! How in the world could you do such a horrible thing! Now what do I do with you sitting in prison for the rest of your life? Didn't you think about me when you when on this crazy spree!? Oh Herb! Why? Why?"

"Yeah, it was stupid of me, but the die is cast now. I won't be long before Detective Dorsey will be here to arrest us."

"Us! Us! Why should I be arrested?"

"Because the detective doesn't know you knew anything of what I have done. Hope they believe me when I tell them you are innocent."

"Herb, you are stupid! I hate to say it!"

"Hey, go pack a suitcase right now. I will too. I have a fake driver's license for both of us. We'll fly to Costa Rica and hide. Go! We haven't a minute to lose!"

"Sweetheart. What kind of a life would that be by constantly running, always looking over our shoulders as to who is behind us. No, that would be a horrible life. But if you wish to go to Costa Rica, go pack and get the hell out of here before the police arrive. It's 10 a.m. You may still have the time. Go pack!"

I went to our bedroom and grabbed a suitcase. Denise followed me and brought out my shaving kit with necessary items from the bathroom. "You do know, that I will file for a divorce on the grounds of desertion. This would give me a chance to remarry and have the children I have always wanted, but you denied me that pleasure because you hate kids."

"I won't contest the divorce you want, Denise. I know you wanted a child or two. Would you do me a big favor? When I leave, take my gun and go to the nearest lake or river and throw it in. Be certain no one sees you doing that. Can you do that for me?"

"You know I hate guns! But if that is what you want done, put it in a plastic grocery sack for me so I don't have to touch it."

"I can do that. Get a plastic sack from the kitchen for me while I finish packing. Meet me by the car in the garage." I snapped the

145

lock on my suitcase and headed for the garage. I thew it in the back seat. Denise came into the garage. I was just about to place my gun in the sack when the doorbell rang. "Good grief! That must be the police or the detective!"

I walked rapidly from the garage into the kitchen and then to the living room. I looked out the door window. There was a large refrigerator size cardboard box next to my porch. "What the hell is all that about?" I opened the door and looked in all directions. I didn't see anybody.

I still had my gun in my hand and walked out on the porch still looking up and down the street. Nothing! *That's weird!*

CHAPTER 55
DETECTIVE MICHAEL

A voice came from the box. "Herbert Pence, why don't you come down to the card board box to meet me as I find a way out of this container. Can you do that for me?"

Herbert walked down the steps to the box, pointing his gun at it, puzzled by the voice coming from the box.

"Herbert Pence. I would highly suggest you lay your gun on the sidewalk and place your hands over your head. There are two policemen, trained as snipers, pointing their rifles at you. If you attempt to shoot, you will be carried away in a body bag. The decision is up to you."

Herb looked down the street and saw the two policemen standing in the bed of a truck with rifles pointing at him.

When Herbert laid his gun on the sidewalk and placed his hands over his head, I came from the side of the house with my gun aimed at Pence. I waved for the two policemen to join me.

"Mr. Pence, you made a wise decision," said Michael.

When the two police arrived with their rifles pointed at Herbert, I pulled his hands down, cuffed him and patted him down. Using my pen, I picked up his .45 Ruger and slid it in a baggie.

One of the police reached into a hole in the box and pulled the radio-mic out and gave it to Michael. After the policemen picked up the box, they carried it to the truck and threw it in the bed and returned to help.

"Did you really think I was in the box knowing you have a happy trigger finger? Just thought I'd follow up on your note on my door. Anything to say about this joke on you? (Pause) Didn't think so. Herbert Pence, you are being arrested for the attempted murder of Tobias Rodriquez, the murder of Lucille Dorsey, and the murder of Tillie Norton. You have the right to remain silent. Anything you say can and will be used against you in a court of law. You have the right to an attorney. If you cannot afford an attorney, one will be appointed for you. Do you understand what I have just said?

"Yeah."

"Is your wife in the house, and if so, is she armed?"

"No, she is not armed. She hates guns. She is innocent and knows nothing about my activities."

"We do not know this for a fact just because you say your wife is innocent. That will be determined later. Bob, put Mr. Pence in my SUV and guard him. Tom, help me do a search of the house after we arrest Mrs. Pence."

We both entered the house cautiously with our guns aimed ahead of us as we entered the living room. Mrs. Pence was sitting on the couch trying to dry her eyes from crying. We holstered are guns.

"Mrs. Pence, please stand." She did and I placed cuffs on her. "Mrs. Pence, you are being arrested as an accomplice to the attempted murder of Tobias Rodriquez, the murder of Lucille Dorsey, my wife incase you didn't know, and of Tillie Norton. Tom, give her her rights."

"Do you understand what was said to you, Mrs. Pence?"

"Yes, I do. My husband killed your wife? Your wife? That's horrible!"

But I'm innocent, Detective. I knew nothing about what Herb had done until he told me shortly before you arrived. I was watching out the window when you arrested him. We were in the garage ready for him to drive to the airport and fly to Costa Rica. Then the doorbell rang."

"I suppose our timing in arriving to arrest you both was bad for you, but good for us. I have a search warrant to locate any incriminating evidence. I see a gun cabinet in your bedroom. Is it locked? If so, do you have the key?"

"It's not locked."

"Good. Tom, take Mrs. Pence to my SUV. Here are my keys. Have Bob take them to headquarters and book them. Also, put them in separate cells. Come back and help me carry out anything we find as evidence I hope you have the keys to the pickup?" He dangled the keys in the air.

I went to the gun cabinet. His arsenal was smaller than expected—a 12-gauge shotgun, a .22 caliber rifle with a scope, a 9mm pistol with a silencer, and the silencer for the .45 caliber gun he surrendered outside. *Silencer-- the reason no one heard any shots at the Walmart murder scene.*

I saw an extra tall wastepaper basket, dumped out the waste paper, and placed all the guns in it along with the boxes of ammunition.

Tom came into the room." Tom, please smooth out those crumpled balls of paper. May be some evidence. Then check the garage for any boxes of papers or possible evidence of Pence's nefarious endeavors. I'm going to check his computer. Hope he didn't use a password."

I booted up the computer. Sure enough, the screen asked for the password. I pulled the computer forward to unhook the various cables. As I was about to unplug the power cable, I saw written on the back plate the words "TVGunsmoke." *Hum-m, that could be his password.*

I booted up the computer again and when entering the password, the computer came alive. I brought up his document file. It was full of correspondence. A quick glance indicated letters sent to drug dealers. *So, our Mr. Pence dealt in drugs too.*

I shut the computer down, pulled the cables and set the computer on the floor ready to be carried to the pickup. Opening the desk drawers, I found seven flash drives. Finding an envelope, I placed them in it and sealed it.

Tom returned from the garage carrying two boxes of files and folders. "Wow, great find. May as well carry them to the pickup.

149

I'll follow with the basket of guns and come back for the computer. Might check the kitchen drawers, the drawers in the bedroom furniture before we leave."

Nothing else was found. The key to the door lock was on a hook by the door. I locked the door, drove back to precinct headquarters where we carried all the items to the forensic computer technicians' lab for examination.

"Tom, thanks for your valuable help, It's 5:30 p.m. It appears we worked overtime. Let's call it a day."

CHAPTER 56
DENISE PENCE

"**M**ay I have an interview with Detective Michael Dorsey regarding the murders he committed?" asked Denise when a staff member brought her meal.

"Captain Rayburn will need to approve that request, Mrs. Pence."

***

The staff member met Detective Tom in the hallway. "Mrs. Pence would desire to have an interview with Detective Dorsey."

Officer Tom went to the captain's office and knocked.

"Come in Tom. "What can I do for you?"

"Mrs. Pence in cell 4 has asked if she can have a conference with Detective Dorsey about her husband's murders."

"That is an unusual request at this early stage of their case. We haven't even asked for any deposition. Yes, ask Detective Dorsey if he is available, and if he can, bring her to our interview room. I want to be present, also."

"Officer Tom went to Detective Michael's office. "Mrs. Pence has indicated that she wants an interview with you now. The captain has approved."

***

Mrs. Pence was facing the captain and Michael. "Thank you for my request for this interview. As soon as possible, I will file for a divorce from Herbert. I do not wish to be married to a murderer, especially that of your wife, Detective Dorsey. I feel so badly about that. When my divorce is finalized, I can testify against my ex-husband. He told me that he murdered Mrs. Dorsey, the women at Walmart and the attempted murder of your brother-in-law. I want to be a witness at his trial and the death penalty for him if possible."

"Mrs. Pence, that is quite a revelation this early of his case," said Captain Rayburn. "We will permit your lawyer to meet in this room. You can take the necessary steps for the divorce."

"Thank you, Captain Rayburn. I have a lawyer. If I can be allowed a phone call, I will set up an appointment with her."

"That is your right. Detective Michael, escort her to your office and accommodate her needs. Again, thank you for being up front with a desire to be a witness," said the captain.

***

Herbert Pence had his arraignment and he stood trial by a jury. There was the strong testimonies by Detective Dorsey, Denise (Pence) Hamilton, her maiden name, Toby's sharing the narrow escape of death and the doctor from the hospital's Sexual Assault Clinic. Pence's lawyer had very weak testimony of three persons whose backgrounds were shown to be questionable by Denise Hamilton's lawyer. The jury was dismissed and met for one hour. They returned with a verdict of guilty of first-degree murder of Lucille Dorsey and of Tillie Norton, and second-degree on the attempted murder of Toby Rodriquez.

One week later when there was no appeal of the verdict, Judge Mark Henson sentenced Herbert Pence to two life time terms in a prison with no opportunity for parole.

***

One year later, Denise Hamilton met a widower, Stanley Newton, with two children—Nathan, age 6, and Natalie, age 4. Denise became a bride and a mother in quick fashion that helped to fulfill her life's dream. However, one year later, she gave birth to a baby boy, Stanley, Jr. She, too, considered herself to have been in the right place at the right time in her life's journey.

CHAPTER 57

TOBY

The cafeteria at Mitchell High was buzzing with the regular overtones of conversation. The Musketeers were eating and chatting about sports and their latest Black Belt sessions. Suddenly, one of the cheerleaders sat down beside Toby.

"Oh, hello Jolene. This is a surprise."

She whispered in Toby's ear. "Would you meet me in the gym at 4:30. I need your help drastically."

Toby fixed his eyes on Jolene's. He quickly sensed that something was affecting her demeanor. "Yes, I can, Jolene. Just me or all four of us?"

"Just you for now," she whispered.

"Okay, Jolene, I'll meet you in the gym," he whispered back.

***

"Thanks for meeting me, Toby. Do you know Robert Meester, Roger Stonelacker, and Charlie Pearson?"

"Yes, I know Robert and Roger very well. They are involved in sports teams along with me and others. I just know who Charlie is."

"I live five blocks from our high school, so I walk most of the time. Those three guys grabbed me last Tuesday and forced me into Robert's car."

"Excuse me, Jolene. I have my tape recorder in my backpack. I use it in my English and History classes to record the teacher's discussions. Let me record what you want me and, possibly, the police to know." He saw her nod of approval, pulled the machine from his backpack, and hit the on button. "Okay, Jolene. What happened?"

"They took me to some abandoned building. Horrible dirty place! There Robert and Roger raped me while Charlie sat on my hands that he pulled over my head. He took picture of those assholes while they raped me."

"Oh Jolene, that is horrible. Absolutely horrible. What did you do or what can you do?"

"When those creeps dropped me off at my home, I immediately told my mother what had happened. She was really upset and angry. My dad was away on a business trip. She took me to the hospital rape clinic. When we arrived, I was in great pain. My underwear and slacks were saturated with blood. Dr. Charlene Bissel gave me a thorough examination. She said that there was much physical trauma to my genitals. She told me that I wouldn't become pregnant. She found the residue that is on the surface of condoms. She will write a detailed summary of her examination that I was definitely sexual assaulted. She indicated that, by law, that her finding must be sent to the authorities. So, they know already. She gave me the name of a rape counselor to help me with the mental anxiety I am experiencing. I have the first session tomorrow."

"Jolene, that was a wise thing to do in getting help."

"That's not all. Now they are threatening me. I need to go with them to that horrible place willingly for more sex or they will sell the pictures to the other guys, telling them I'm a whore. They had to have sold a picture to Mike Benson, who showed me the horrible picture and asked me for a date. I knew what he had in mind and told him 'no' quickly. It's Friday. I know Robert is waiting for me to come out of the front door now. Let's go to that window at the top of the bleachers. It overlooks the parking lot."

We climbed the steps and looked out the window. True to her words, Roger and Charlie were leaning against Robert's car. "They are waiting for Robert to force me to his car."

"Jolene, this is a criminal case. This is way beyond what the Musketeers can possibly handle to help you. You need to go to the police with this terrible situation."

"I can't do that, Toby. They have threatened me that if I go to the police, they have paid another person who will kill me so I can't testify against them."

"Wow. They really have you tied in knots, Jolene."

"It's terrible! I can't eat with out vomiting. I can't sleep. I can't keep my mind on my studies. It's a real nightmare for me. I was relieved to know I couldn't get pregnant. Toby, I don't know what to do! I'm at my wit's end!"

"Jolene, my brother-in-law is a detective with the Aroura Police Department. I'll give him the tape to listen and to know what happened. He may just know how to handle this situation you're in without endangering you anymore than you are now and get those three creeps arrested. He may already have seen the report of the doctor." I turned the recorder off.

"Oh, Toby, that would be so great!"

"Why don't you wait by the door on the other side of the gym. That door is next to the circular driveway. I'll drive around in front to see if Robert is waiting. I'll go around the block and come up the driveway. I'll give a short touch on my horn for you to get in the back seat and lie down. You can direct me on the streets to your house."

"Toby, I truly thank you. You are a good friend."

"I'll do what I can, Jolene."

***

Toby went to the parking lot. Roger and Charlie were leaning against Robert's car.

"Hey, Toby, school has been out for some time. Where have you been?" asked Roger.

"Hi guys. I had to help a student with a problem."

"Did you see Jolene Thompson, per chance?" asked Roger.

"Why, are you taking her home? She lives four blocks from school, doesn't she? Probably stayed after school for some reason. See ya!"

The plan worked without a hitch. I had Jolene at her home in no time.

As Jolene exited the car, she said, "Toby, you are a life saver."

"We'll do the same ruse next week, if necessary, Jolene. I'm happy to help you."

CHAPTER 58
DETECTIVE MICHAEL

I called the Rodriquez family early on Monday morning. "Greta, I'll be by this morning to pick up Toby. If you and Henry have no objection, my lawyer, Patrick Flanigan, and the District Attorney, Marsha Blackburn, need a deposition from Toby and to prepare the case for trial of Pence's attempted murder when it comes up on the docket. We are doing some preliminary work on my own case against Pence on the death of Lucille."

"Mike, thank you for the help. Let us know the cost of your lawyer. Henry, being a divorce lawyer, can't be of much help. He may wish to be present in your sessions, however. Unfortunately, he left for Lakewood early this morning on a very sticky divorce settlement."

"Yes, that's true that his expertise in divorces is far different from murder cases. When the conference is over, I'll drive Toby to the car shop. The windows have been replaced. The car insurance policy was in the glove compartment. They will bill your insurance company for the balance after the deductible has been subtracted."

"Again, thank you, Mike, for all you do for us."

***

Toby entered Mike's car. "This is a real surprise, Mike. How long will this session take?"

"I really can't say exactly. Probably two hours. As I told your mother, I'll take you to the car repair after the session. They called that your windows have been replaced."

"That's super. Glad to get my car back. Using Mother's car forced her to use the city bus to get to work. She will be as happy as I am."

***

"Toby, you were really on the ball during the conference. The DA shared with me that you were far more knowledgeable about the entire discussion and tentative plans for the jury trial than many adult clients. We may have more sessions later when the case comes up to be held."

"Glad to do my part, Mike. Before you take me to the shop, can we go to your office. I need your advice or help on another bad situation."

Toby pulled out his recorder from his backpack and turned it on. Mike listened intensely to Jolene's story.

"Toby, that poor young lady! The captain may have already received the sexual assault report from the hospital. I'll share more of Jolene's horrible problem with this recording. We'll come up with a plan to arrest these rapists with as little fanfare as possible. This will help minimize the danger to the victim. Do you know these students?"

"Oh, yes. Robert and Roger are involved with me in several sports teams. They are all seniors. I know who Charlie is also."

"Good! Let's get your car and you can be on your way to school for part of a day. Hope you don't have too much makeup work."

"Hope not either. I do know I have a short test to make up with my history teacher."

"You'll ace it, Toby."

Toby shot a glance at Mike. He was grinning from ear to ear.

"Mike, you're too much. But I love you as if you were truly my brother."

CHAPTER 59

TOBY

W hen I entered the cafeteria on Tuesday lunch hour, I spotted Detectives Michael and Tom standing along the outside walls near the tables of the rival street gang students. Michael saw Toby sitting at his table and moved slowly along the perimeter wall until he was close to the table. He motioned for Toby to come to him. "Can you point out these three characters we need to watch? Tom and I have been approved by the school board president and the principal as substitute staff. I have shared Jolene Thompson's dilemma with him. He was appalled to hear what happened."

"I will sit down beside them for I have a message for Robert. I can see that they are sitting together on the edge of their table."

"Great. I'll be a short distance away." He motioned for Tom to move closer to him.

I picked up my tray and went to the three students. "Can you make room for me Robert? The coach gave me a message to give you."

"Now what did I do or what didn't I do?" asked Robert.

"Well, he asked me to tell you that you still have football equipment you haven't turned in as yet."

"Oh crap! The coach is always on my ass. I haven't had the time yet to clean out my locker of football stuff. I guess I better do it soon."

"Good idea, Robert. Two seniors last year did not clean out their lockers. They had to pay $400 each for all the gear before getting their diplomas."

"Wow! Best I get my butt in motion then. Thanks for giving me a warning. Hey, Roger and Charlie, I need to use the john and pee. Why don't you dump your trays and meet me in the john. We can share a hit before the bell rings for class."

CHAPTER 60
DETECTIVES MICHAEL AND TOM

I studied Robert's actions. He appeared slightly agitated. When he left the cafeteria, I slowly followed him at a safe distance. When Robert entered the boys' toilet, I briefly delayed going in.

At the moment Robert saw me enter, he said, "The faculty toilet is down the hallway and to the right."

"Oh, okay. This is my first day in this building and no one told me about the faculty lounge and toilet. I got to pee, so excuse the intrusion."

"Okay, I guess," said Robert. He lit up a marijuana cigarette and took a big drag.

Tom watched the other two leave and go by the table of cheerleaders. Roger stopped and waved an envelope in the air. Tom surmised that his actions were directed as a threat to their victim. As the two left the cafeteria, I saw them dashing toward the boys' toilet and followed them in.

"Good grief! We're being invaded by first time subs! Didn't anyone tell you people about the faculty lounge? Jeepers!" said Robert. He gave his hit to Roger who took a big draw and then handed it to Charlie who also made a draw and handed the butt back to Robert.

I washed my hands. "Do you students smoke weed here every day? The place really reeks of marijuana. If you use it, you undoubtedly sell it. Right?"

"If you don't tell anyone, Roger and I have extras." Both pulled a plastic bag from their jean's pocket and held the contents up high. "There is enough to get a real buzz if that is what you wish to experience," said Robert.

Michael pulled out his billfold and removed a twenty. "What's your selling price?"

"Twenty is fine," said Robert, as he pulled a roll up from the bag and gave one to Michael while pocketing the money. Tom produced a twenty and gave it to Roger, who in turn, gave him a roll up.

Robert drew the last drag, threw the butt in the sink, turned on the faucet and watched it flush down the drain.

Both detectives moved near the door. They pulled out their badges and showed them to the three students whose eyes bugged and mouths dropped open. "In addition to being substitute staff today, we are also police with the Aurora Police Department. You three are being arrested for the use and sale of drugs on school property that is against its rules and regulations."

Both detectives pulled out a set of handcuffs, pulled Robert's and Roger's hands behind their backs and snapped on the cuffs. Charlie, seeing this happening, made a beeline for the door, only to run smack dab into another student who had entered. Both ended in a heap on the floor. Tom pulled another set of cuffs and snapped the cuffs together of Robert and Roger. Michael rolled Charlie over on his stomach, pulled his hands behind his back, snapped on the cuffs, then helped him to his feet. The other student jumped up and made a bee line out the door.

Both detectives showed their badges again. "Roger," asked Tom, "Is that envelope in your back pocket the same one you waved in the air for someone to assume was a signal or warning? Would you show it to me?"

Roger pulled the envelope out of his pocket with his cuffed hand, backed up, and held it for the detective to take it. Tom pulled out the contents. "These are pictures of a female victim being sexual assaulted, aren't they?"

"We know all the details of your rape of Jolene Thompson. In addition to your drug charges, you are being arrested for the sexual assault of one female student. You each have the right to remain silent. Anything you say can and will be used against you in a court of law. You have the right to an attorney. If you or your parents can't afford an attorney, one will be appointed for you. Do you understand what I have stated?" asked Michael.

All three mumbled out, "Yes, I do."

"We are taking you to our precinct headquarters, booked, and your parents notified to come to our precinct along with their lawyers as soon as possible," said Michael. "There are more charges, but these will be given when your parents and lawyers are present."

The three were ushered to Michael's SUV. "Tom, these guys are in your charge while I inform the principal of their arrest."

CHAPTER 61
CAPTAIN E. J. RAYBURN AND DISTRICT ATTORNEY MARSHA BLACKBURN

"Good evening, folks. I thank you for being present," said Captain Rayburn. "I regret that you had to arrange your schedule to be present for this important preliminary meeting. We need to know who is present. Mr. and Mrs. Daniel Meester." They raised their hands. "Your son is Robert and your attorney is Sidney Watson. Hi, Sid, haven't seen you for some time. Mr. and Mrs. A. J. Stonelacker." They acknowledged the captain. "Your son is Roger and your attorney is Glen Cameron. Mrs. Janet Pearson and your son is Charlie. You requested that an attorney be appointed for you. She is Sandra Downing." Sandra shook hands with Mrs. Pearson, and with Charlie."

"You three young men did not, unfortunately, think clearly when you sexually assaulted your victim. She may be scarred for the rest of her life. She is being counseled now. This may help significantly. As for the charges being brought against you, they will be presented now by District Attorney Marsha Blackburn. Also present are Detectives Michael Dorsey and Tom Dillard, both of whom you three young men have already met."

Marsha stood up and studied the faces of the three young men and of their parents for several moments. The concerned appearances of grim faces were most apparent.

"I have the detailed reports of both detectives as to the use and sale of drugs on school property which is prohibited by the schools' own rules and regulations. I have listened to a recording of the victim who verbalized the horrible situation she is suffering now as a result of what you three young men did and the threats made. When you were booked and asked to remove all items from your pockets, Robert and Roger, you had in your possession vials of cocaine. Under Colorado state law, the open and public display, consumption, or use of marijuana, except as provided by the emergency reporting exception, is a drug petty offense if the amount is two ounces or less, and is punishable by a fine of up to $100 and/or 24 hours of community service. As for the unlawful use of cocaine, this is a Colorado level two drug misdemeanor which carries up to 12 months in jail, and/or $50 to $750 in fines. However, the court may instead impose the lighter penalty for drug use."

Mrs. Pearson raised her hand. "Charlie tells me he doesn't buy or sell marijuana, only takes a draw now and then when offered by Robert or Roger. How serious is that?"

"Have Sandra discuss that situation. She knows the Colorado law also."

"I have the report of the detectives arresting you on the charges of sexual assault of a high school female student. I have in hand the report of the examination of the victim by the sexual assault clinic at General Hospital. Dr. Charlene Bissel can testify at your trial of her detailed findings. The detectives located the abandoned building and the space were the assault happened. They found a pool of blood. They were able to gather a specimen for a blood test. It was a positive match to that of the victim. Colorado law, 18-3-402 states that the survivor of a sexual assault is never to blame. The person or persons responsible is the perpetrator of the crime. Based on information gathered, this is a class four felony leaving defendants facing 2 to 8 years in jail followed by a three-year parole. Fines can range from $2,000 to $50,000."

"Charges relative to your production and sale of pornographic material leading to prostitution and/ or solicitation is covered by

Colorado law 18-7-201. Fines can be up to $300 and up to 10 days in jail."

"Colorado law 18-3-206 defines the crime of menacing using threats or action knowingly to place or an attempt to place another person in fear of imminent serious bodily injury or death—the offense can be charged as a misdemeanor or a felony and is punishable by up to three years in prison. You three young men threatened your victim that a fourth person was paid to murder your victim so she could not testify against you. What we need immediately is the name and address of this person so he or she is removed from committing this crime. We will use five minutes for you three attorneys to solicit the information needed."

"Time has expired. What is the name and address of the assassin?"

Sidney Watson stood up. "My client indicated no one was hired to murder the victim. The threat was used to force the victim to remain silent about the sexual assault."

Glen Cameron stood up. "My client indicated the same answer that Robert Meester gave."

Sandra Downing stood up. My client is not aware of any threat. He states that the threat must have been made when he was not present."

"There is a large problem with your answers. The victim is living under the dire threat to this minute. We will need to inform the victim. I am advising you three students that what you told your attorneys is not the truth and the victim is murdered, we will need to find the assassin and you two students who gave the order to eliminate the victim will be subject to additional penalties for second- or third-degree murder and subject to be in prison for a longer period of time in addition to the charges already made. All this is to help you three young men realize the import of your actions. Any questions. (Pause) If none, your attorneys may now meet for a half hour with your clients and parents. You can arrange for more conferences as needed at this time also."

"May I have your attention again. Thank you. I am certain your attorneys informed you that each will have an arraignment at a court hearing, which will be your first appearance in court. If your actions are deemed as a criminal case, it makes one of the initial stages in the pretrial process. During the hearing, the judge will inform you, as the defendant, of the charges filed against you and will be asked how you, the accused, plead to those charges. Again, your lawyer will certainly help you to understand these procedures which will be very new to you. I am finished, Captain."

The captain stood up. "We realize that you three young men have around three months for graduation. Since you will be denied bail to protect the life of your victim, we have made arrangements for you to continue your education while incarcerated. Detective Dorsey will add to his collateral duties the supervision of your studies. Toby Rodriquez, that you three know rather well, is being added to our staff. He will be the go between and will bring your books and will be in touch with your teachers, who will outline the curriculum which you will need to follow until the last days of school. Toby will gather your homework and submit it to your teachers. Any quizzes or final test will be given to Detective Dorsey. Graduation day has been set for May 20th. Based on your behavior, progress and passing of your final tests, arrangements will be made to join your classmates on graduation day if you so desire. More details will be provided as time progresses. Are there any questions? Yes, Mr. Meester."

"Will the boys be able to have physical education? Robert, and I know Roger also, do physical training with fitness equipment. Will they be able to maintain that training while in jail?"

"Definitely. We do have a fitness room which the police and staff use to stay fit for their duties. Detective Dorsey will add that as part of their daily routine. When the weather is suitable again, we do have a partial basketball court to use. Any more questions? (Pause) If not, you lawyers may continue consultation with your client and parents as long as you wish. Good night to each of you."

***

The three defendants had been through the arraignment process where the attorneys had advised each to plead not guilty.

The case for each was settled out of court.

The District Attorney, Marsha Blackburn, met with the defendant, the parents, and their attorney in the following days.

In the case of Charlie Pearson with his appointed lawyer, Sandra Downing, and by plea bargaining, he was sentenced to one year in prison. It was suspended based on future behavior. He was given 60 days of community service. It would be necessary for him to report to the APD each day from 9a.m. to 4p.m. to assist the janitor in the cleaning and maintenance of the precinct headquarters.

Robert Meester was sentenced to two years in prison and a fine of $35,000 plus one year of supervised parole upon released by plea bargaining with Sidney Watson as his lawyer.

Roger Stonelacker by plea bargaining with his lawyer, Glen Cameron, was sentenced to two years in prison followed by one year of supervised parole and a fine of $30,000.

Both Robert and Roger were informed that the reason for the minimum of two years of prison time was for their serious threat of death of their victim.

CHAPTER 62

TOBY

I arrived at the parking lot of the hardware store where I work. The lot in front of the store was full. I drove around the back of the store to a lot on the right side of the store. As I drove around the back, I saw two men sitting on the ground leaning against the trash bin. I thought, *a couple of guys sleeping off a drunken stupor.*

I parked and walked back to the men. I hollered, Hello! Wake up guys!" There was no response. I placed my fingers on the carotid artery of one person. No pulse. I did the same on the second person. No pulse. *Wow! Two dead men on our property.*

I pulled out my cellphone and punched in the number for Detective Michael's office.

"Detective Dorsey's office. This is Sally. How may I help you?"

"This is Toby. May I speak with Mike?"

"I'm sorry Toby, he is not in his office at the present time. He told me he would be back in a short—oh, he just walked into the office. Here, Toby is on the line."

"Hi Toby, what's up this time?"

"Mike, there are two dead men behind our Ace Hardwar Store leaning against a trash bin. I found no pulse on either one."

"Thanks Toby. We'll take over from there. Can you stay with the corpses until we get there?"

"Mike, I need to be at work at nine. I don't want to be late. I can't wait that long."

"Okay Toby. I understand. Tell Mr. Johnson what you discovered behind his store. He will certainly be concerned and go to the place until we arrive."

"I'll tell him, Mike."

***

Detective Dorsey, a policeman, the forensic team, the coroner, an ambulance, and two EMTs arrived within fifteen minutes.

The coroner checked the men's arms. Many scars were apparent from dozens of needle insertions. "I would say they died from an overdose. Our forensic team at the morgue will be able to determine what drugs caused their death. We are having a rash of these deaths."

The forensic team took pictures of the men. They searched the whole area. One climbed into the trash bin and scoured among the trash. Nothing was found that would be beneficial to help solve the death of the men.

"They could have been drugged someplace else and then dumped here," offered one EMT.

"I would agree," replied Detective Dorsey.

The EMT's placed the men on stretchers and rolled them to the ambulance. Everyone left except Michael. He entered the store with Mr. Johnson. He noticed Toby arranging garden products and placing more merchandise on the shelves.

"Thanks, Toby, for finding those men. Again, you were in the right place at the right time to find them."

"Well, if the truth be known, had the parking lot in front not been full, I would not have driven around the store to the other lot and would not have found them."

"Of course, we may have discovered them when taking out rubbish later in the day."

"I need to get back to my office. My supervisor wants us to get a handle on all the victims with large injections of drugs. I won't be a bit surprise that these two men fit in that category also."

CHAPTER 63
DETECTIVE DORSEY

"**T**his is the Aurora Police Headquarters. How may I direct your call?"

"This is the Aldman Motel at 560 Corral Road, here in Aurora. Housekeeping found two men dead in their bed a few minutes ago, room 12. Would you send the police immediately?"

"Yes, I will. Your name for contact purposes?"

"I'm Johnny Schroeder, the owner."

"I'll inform the officers immediately."

"Thank you. They can't get here too soon for our benefit."

***

Sally called Detective Dorsey that she knew was in his office.

"Yes, Sally, what's up this time?"

"I just received a call from a Johnny Schroeder at the Aldman Motel, 560 Corral Road here in Aurora. Housekeeping found two dead men in Room 12 and desire to have them removed immediately."

Michael knew that the captain was not in his office, so he went to the Police Commissioner's office. He knocked on his door.

"Come in, Detective. What great weight is on your shoulders?"

I relayed the information of the four dead men.

"What the hell is happening, Detective? We are experiencing a rash of dead men and women these days. We had a call to remove two men found dead in an apartment on the Southside of Aurora. There was a call to remove two men found dead in a trailer park on the north side. The men were full of drugs. All four were injected with a walloping dose of methamphetamine. The bodies were stripped of any ID. Now this. Here are the reports from the forensic lab so far. I want you and the other detectives to work these cases and find some rhyme or reason for all these deaths and who might be behind them. We arrested a Kenneth Brown, age 47, and his daughter, Janice Waters, 29, who were distributing crack cocaine. The two had given out over 450 grams of the stuff by conducting around 955 drug-related transactions during a five-month period right here in the Aurora area. This Brown person already has a record. He has been charged on the state level with possession of crack, marijuana, and ecstasy and drug paraphernalia in connection with his arrest in November 2020. The daughter was indicted in federal court in December 2020 for the conspiracy to distribute controlled substances. She was sentenced January, 2021, for eight months in prison and three years of supervised release. But she and her dad just reverted back immediately to what they determine would make them rich. I can't believe these two are behind all these deaths, however. What is strange is the fact that there are two men in each of these death situations."

"I agree with you that we have a real problem with drugs. But I better be on my way."

"Gosh, yes! I've been bending your ears long enough. I'll call the coroner, forensic team and an ambulance to meet you at the motel. Give me your findings on this case as soon as you can."

"I'll do just that, Commissioner."

CHAPTER 64
DETECTIVES DORSEY AND TOM DILLARD

We sat at a table pouring over the forensic reports of the eight deaths. We found the report at the Aldman Motel had finger print found on the door frame. The print belonged to a Stephanie Hamilton, from LaJunta, Colorado. We couldn't find any information about her being a drug user or of her selling it. We concluded that she had been a guest at the motel prior to the dead men being found there. We discovered that no name was given or money was paid for the room from the owner's records. He had no answers to that puzzling situation.

Fingerprints of the deceased were used to identify everyone. The reports indicated all the victims' pockets were cleaned out of any material. It was revealing that all had prior records of felonies and misdemeanors. We were able to reach some members of their family for seven individuals. We found no missing reports had been made for any of the victims. All contacts indicated that the men were gay and part of the LGBTQ community. We scrutinized every photograph that had been taken for clues. The blood toxicology reports of all eight men indicated large doses of methamphetamine and then placed or dumped where they were found. We were drawing the conclusion that another person or persons had a hatred or vendetta for the life style of these black men. Now comes the task of finding that person or persons in the wide universe. We were just hoping against hope that something would give us a break.

***

Two days later, we had an anonymous call to the precinct of a tip that an Edward Blankenship could be a person of interest in killing of gay men. We entered the name into our criminal name base. He was five feet nine inches, 165 pounds, 37 years old, Caucasian, and last address was 1636 Small Street, Aurora.

"Les's make a visit to this address, Tom. May lead to something that could surprise us," said Michael.

"Yes, in our work one lead may turn into another that we desperately need," replied Tom.

Arriving at the address, they found the house to be a small white and blue trimmed bungalow. Michael rang the doorbell.

Ayoung woman answered the door with a small child clinging to her skirt.

"I'm Detective Dorsey and this is Detective Dillard. We are trying to locate Edward Blankenship. Our information indicated that he lives at this address," said Michael.

The lady looked at both of us suspiciously. "Why do you need him?"

"He may be involved in some suspicious activities," stated Tom. "We want to clear his name if our information is in error."

"He did live here. He sold us this house for a small price. We couldn't believe our good luck. He even left us his furnishings, also. We borrowed the money to pay him. He left and said he needed to start over someplace else in the United States. He kept repeating words to that affect for some time, then entered his car and sped away."

"Any indication where he was going? Stay in Aurora or move out of state? asked Michael.

"I had the reaction that he was going out of state."

"When did you purchase this house from him?" asked Michael.

"It will be two weeks tomorrow."

"Any mail that is still coming to this address" asked Michael.

"Yes, yes, two letters did arrive today. I need to place them on my mailbox to be picked up tomorrow."

"May I have them to take to the post office? I can ask them if he left a forwarding address," said Michael.

"Yes, I'll get them from the kitchen shelf." She returned quickly.

"Here they are. Good luck finding my generous benefactor."

"Thank you for your help, The post office may have some information for us," said Michael.

***

We drove to the post office. Talking to a lady at one of the windows and sharing our needs, she brought up the screen for Edward Blankenship. "I'm sorry to inform you, he did not leave any forwarding address. We have been returning the letters he received back to the senders."

"Thank you for the assistance," said Michael.

"Guess that's a dead end for us," said Tom.

"Let's return to our offices and study the forensic reports again on the eight victims, replied Michael. "We may have missed something that may help us. We can contact the DMV and ask for a search of his car."

***

"I'll call the DMV," said Michael. He jotted down the information that was given him. He turned to Tom. "Edward drives a 2021 Legacy Subaru. Plates are GRS431, and in the one-month grace period to be renewed. I'll have an all-points bulletin sent out to find the car. How let's comb these reports for more possible leads."

CHAPTER 65
EDWARD BLANKENSHIP AKA HOWARD JENNINGS

need to slide under the radar. The police have found those eight stupid gay men that I put out of their misery by now. I covered my tracks so they can't find any leads to me. I just need to outwit those dicks. I need to stay ahead of them and use my common sense and smarts. I'll go to California, find a community that will help me get lost, using cash for all transactions. Selling my house for cash placed me in a good position to do just that.

But how can I get anywhere. By plane? No, their records could nail me. Bus? Might be possible. You buy a ticket and no record of transaction. Driving my car is too risky. They will put out an all-points bulletin on my car. I'm bound to be caught.

I sat in my chair nursing a beer while mentally brainstorming. I need a good alternative. What if I steal a car, change plates with another car. That could get me to California in three days and before the owners would realize what took place before notifying the cops. I'll ditch my car some way.

I drove to a respectable neighborhood near where I did live—Maple Street. I parked and observed the activities of the residents. Couple of men were mowing their lawns. A woman was working on a flower bed. Suddenly, an elderly lady drove past my car and pulled into a drive way. I watched as she unloaded sacks from her car and carried them into her house. She made two trips. Then she drove the car into the garage. Hm-m. A 2015 four-door Dodge. That may just be the car to get me to California. Probably low mileage. Good condition. I'll come back at eleven o'clock and break in. Hot-wire it and drive away. I'll stop and switch plates with another car. Get rid of my car and be on my way. Sounds like an ideal plan. Then I saw a bus go past me. Ah, yes, that's how I'll get back here tonight.

I drove to Cherry Creek Basin and parked. There were some fishermen along the bank.

They never notice me. I walked back to the main road and started walking and holding out my thumb. A truck driver stopped for me.

"How far are you going, Pal?" as he stopped and spoke to me from his window.

"Downtown Aurora would be great."

"You're in luck, Pal. I'm headed to Home Depot to buy lumber."

I pulled myself up into his cab. "I do appreciate stopping for me. My buddy is fishing and plans to stay late into the evening. I was tired of waiting and wanted to get back home. Fish were not biting anyway."

"That can be a problem. Some days are great and others are a waste of time. Don't have much time to fish. Need to work every day to put food on the table for my family."

We arrived at the Depot. We both exited the truck. "Thanks for the lift. Really appreciate your stopping for me. The best to you and your family."

"You are certainly welcome. Thanks for your company."

I walked to a bus stop. When the first bus stopped, I asked the driver which bus would take me to Maple Street. He circled the bus line on a map and gave it to me. "Thanks for the directions."

I entered a restaurant nearby and ordered a meal. It was 5:30 p.m. I had some time to burn before taking a bus to Maple Street. I memorized the bus schedule I needed to use. I bought a newspaper and looked for any news items about the men I put out of their misery. Nothing.

At 9:30, I took the Grant Park bus. I received a bus transfer that would take me to the block of the lady's car. I asked the bus driver to stop opposite the lady's house. He was most obliging.

When I exited the bus, the driver said." This is the last bus run for this time of the night for this area."

"Oh, that's okay. I have other plans. Thanks.".

The lights were on so I surmised that she had already retired. I tried the garage door. It was locked. I put my shoulder against the door and the lock gave way. *Sorry lady to split the door frame.* I pulled out my cellphone and turned on the flashlight. The car door was not locked. When I got behind the wheel, I couldn't believe my luck. She had left the keys in the ignition switch. I got out of the car and tripped the switch to open the garage door. I backed the car out, returned to close the garage door, backed out to the street and was on my way. *So far, so good.*

I drove three blocks when I spotted an older car in the street. I backed up and parked behind it. I looked about the area. I saw no one. Using a pliers and a screw driver, I removed the plates from both vehicles. I switched plates in no time. The street lights help me also. I was soon on my way. Seeing the gas gauge close to empty. I stopped at a Chevron station, filled the tank and paid the attendant cash. *So far, so good.*

I happily drove my stolen vehicle to the Cherry Creek Basin and parked beside my car. I checked to see if anybody was doing any night fishing. I found no one. *Again, so far, so good!*

I moved my two suitcases from my car to Mrs. X's. Then I backed my car 25 yards from the edge of the basin. I removed my plates. Breaking the windshield with a rock and using my cellphone light, I used my screwdriver to pry loose the VIN number. That was far more difficult than I thought it would. I finally succeeded. I placed the VIN number and plates in a grocery bag, placed a dozen rocks in, tied a knot, walked to the basin and tossed it in the water, thinking that it would sink into the dirt and silt. Walking back to my car, I broke a yard stick long enough to wedged between the accelerator and the car cushion. I reached in and started the motor which immediately roared wide open. I pushed the shifting lever into high. The front wheels began to squeal as traction took place. As the car shot forward, the edge of the door scraped my right shoulder and threw me forcefully to the road. I could see my car go down the lane and over the bank. I got up and ran to the edge and watched my car sink out of sight. It would be wise to get rid of my cellphone, too, so they can't trace me, and with that decision, tossed it as far s possible. *Ah yes, so far, so good.*

With a slightly sore shoulder, I got into my stolen prize and headed for I-25 highway that would begin my journey. I drove to Santa Fe and arrived at day break. I was tired physically and emotionally, so I pulled into the first motel I saw, registered with my fictious name, paid cash and found my room. I really do not remember placing my head on the pillow. I slept until noon, thanking myself to have presence of mind to have set the alarm clock.

After a long shower, I put on my same clothes, checked out, and headed for Albuquerque. I did stop at a gas station to fill the tank. When paying for the gas, I picked up a sack of donuts and a bottle of orange juice. That would be my noon meal as I continued driving and eating. The "borrowed car" was a pleasure to drive. I noticed that my heavy foot brought me over the speed limit, so I found the cruise control settings and turned it on. I don't wish to be stopped for speeding. I noticed the speedometer dial showed 30,467 miles. The car is hardly broken in.

I cruised down I-40 highway with a stop at Albuquerque to top off the gas tank and buy some snacks to help prevent road hypnosis. I drove until midnight, stopping at a motel in Flagstaff. Again, I was tired beyond a capacity to think intelligently and must have scared the clerk who gave me a key to my room. Again, I fell into a death stage sleep when I finally slid under the covers. Somehow, I did set my alarm clock for noon.

The next morning was bright and shining. After breakfast in a nearby café, I topped the tank with gas, hoping to make Los

Angeles late that day. I did. Finding a motel, I crashed and slept until two p.m.

I did the usual morning ritual of shaving and showering. I dressed in clean clothes from my suitcase. When I had been wearing were very ripe. *Need to find a laundry. Also buy new threads to fit in with California styles.*

I went to the office lounge and found the Los Angeles Times. I turned to the ads to find apartments for rent or lease. I wrote down the addresses of those that piqued my interest and location in or around L.A. Using the computer for guest, I looked up the addresses and made copies of the directions.

The first one was in Torrance. Following the printed maps, I found my way to the apartment building. It was attractive enough. *I hope there are open rentals.* Finding the office, I entered a richly furnished office. The office secretary greeted me. "May I help you? You are in luck for we have three vacancies."

"That's super. May I eyeball each to make a choice?"

"You certainly may." She pushed a button on her desk. Another smartly dressed lady approached me. "I'm Anita Billings," She offered me her right hand. "Thanks for considering Harmon's Apartments. Follow me." The elevator stopped on the third floor. "We have two vacancies on this floor and one on the second." She opened 310.

When I stepped in, the total space had an inviting sensation. The dining/living area was well furnished. She led me to the small kitchen. She pointed to the bed room. It was well furnished also. The entire place was inviting and more adequate than I could imagine.

"I'll take it. What are your rates for three months payment at a time. Is there a break in the cost?"

"Yes, there is, but that can be easily worked out with the manager you met in the office."

"Do you accept cash? I haven't had time to establish a bank account. *Wasn't planning to do that anyway.*

"Yes, we accept cash. I assume you want this apartment?"

"This is suitable for my needs. The furnishings are excellent. I'll need to do some shopping for bedding, toiletry items, and groceries. What store do you recommend for these purchases?"

"There is a Walmart store on Hawthorne, not too far from here. You can purchase everything in one stop."

"Your advice is as worthy as your beauty, Anita. I'm Howard Jennings. Let's get the rent out of the way before I go shopping. I need to settle down and enjoy this sunshine and all the amenities in the area. Thank you for your part in the beginning of my adventures."

CHAPTER 66

MRS. AGNES UNDERWOOD

"**I**'m so sorry Hobo that I ran out of food for you. You are not a happy kitty cat. But now you're hungry and no food. I'll go to the store right now."

Grabbing my purse, I went to the garage. I found the door open and the wood split. *Who did that?* Then I saw that my car was gone. "Somebody stole my Rambo!" I shouted out loud.

Returning to my house, I dialed the Aurora Police station. After telling them of my missing car, I was informed that a police officer would make a visit very shortly to acquire more information.

Sergeant Edwards arrived in half an hour. I was very upset and nervous. "What information can you give me, Mrs. Underwood, so we can place an all-points bulletin to help recover it?"

"Let me think. It is a four door 2015 Dodge, Journey model, I believe, a rather sporty car for my age, but I loved it. Don't remember the license plate numbers."

"That's okay. We can obtain that information from DMV. When was the last time you drove your car."

"Ah, that would be three days ago."

"That's not good information. The thief could be a long distance from Aurora, unless it's still in the area. Do you carry the registration in the car?"

"Yes, in the glove apartment. Oh wait. I may have last year's receipt. I'll try to find it."

"While you do that, Mrs. Underwood, I'll check the garage for any visual help." I studied the door. He must have hit it with his foot or a shoulder to have split the wood where the lock entered the door frame. I pulled out my finger print dusting bag from my shirt pocket. Dusting the metal areas, I found many finger prints with no one outstanding to use. No help here. I returned to the house.

"Sorry, Mr. Policeman. I can't find it."

"That's okay. I can acquire the information from DMV. What color was your car?"

"Brown or dark tan."

"I'll download a picture of that model that will be helpful for the all-points bulletin."

"I hope you can find it, Officer. Guess I will need to use the bus now."

"We'll do our level best to find it, Mrs. Underwood."

"Thank you, Officer."

CHAPTER 67
RANDY LAWRENCE

Good grief! My car is filthy dirty from driving on those gravel roads two days ago. Need to wash it to be more respectable. I parked it on my lawn so the water used would have double use.

As I hosed off the dust from all sides, I glanced at my license plates. *Those aren't my plates, or are they? My plates didn't start with SKY?* I laid the hose down and proceeded to get the registration receipt from the house. When comparing the plate numbers, those on my car were different. "What the Sam hill is happening? How long has these plates been on my Chevy?' I said out loud.

I finished hosing off the dust, turned off the water, parked back on the street, and dried off the water with towels. I proceeded to remove the plates. With the plates and my registration receipt, I drove to the DMV with my wife's car.

***

I gave the plates and receipt to a woman whose name plate read Marcella in window five when my number was called. She brought up my plate numbers that were on my car. "Those plates belong to a Mrs. Underwood. Someone switched plates and yours are being used by someone else, apparently. I'll notify the Aurora Police Department of this situation. I will issue you a new pair of plates for your car, along with a new registration receipt."

"Do I need to pay for new plates?"

"No, you don't. You have five months before you need to renew the new plates."

"Thank you. I wonder who has Mrs. Underwood's car with my plates?"

CHAPTER 68
MARCELLA SIBLEY WITH THE DMV

I dialed the number for the APD.

"This is Sally at the APD. How may I help you?"

"This is Marcella Sibley with the Department of Motor Vehicles. We have another situation where someone has removed the plates, SKY609, belonging to Mrs. Agnes Underwood, and placed on Randy Lawrence's car. His plate number is JTL845. I suspect that someone has Mrs. Underwood's car with Randy Lawrence's plates. Our department has records of this happening many times."

"Thank you, Marcella. I have the information. I'll give it to one of our detectives. May prove to be helpful for them."

"Glad to be of help."

CHAPTER 69

JOE JOHNSON

What a great day for fishing! Those fish are just waiting for me at Cherry Creek Basin. Friend called last night that those trout are biting on lures at the lower end of the basin.

I found six fishermen already there. "Are you catching anything?"

"Yep," one answered. Have four in my ice chest."

I cast my favorite lure that had been successful on other trips. Slowly reeling in the lure, I had a snag. "Damnit. My first cast and I get a snag. That's a $14 lure," I complained to the nearest fisherman.

"What are you going to do? Cut the line?"

"Hell no! I don't see any women here. I'm going in to unsnag it." I proceeded to strip down to my shorts, removed my shoes and socks and jumped into the water. It was cold. I followed my line where it entered the water and down to the snag. I couldn't believe my eyes. A car, a Subaru!

I pushed off from the roof of the car to fill my lungs with oxygen again. I dived down and found the hook embedded in the crack of the trunk lid. I unhooked it and threw the lure clear of the car. I pushed myself back to the surface, swam to the bank, and climbed out.

"Would you believe that there is a car submerged at the bottom of the basin?" I said to the fishermen nearest me.

"No kidding? So that was your big catch of the day? The fisherman jokingly said.

I wicked the water from my body with my hand, then dried off with a towel from my tackle box. I finished dressing. I better call the police."

I walked back to my fishing rod and begin winding the reel. As I did, I felt a pull on the line. I flipped my rod up to set the hook. By George, I have one! I continued reeling in the line. I lifted and flipped a 12-inch Rainbow trout onto the bank. Grabbing it, I removed the hook and dumped it in my bucket of water.

"How about my luck! Finding a car in the water and reeling in a big one," I shouted to the other fisherman. I fished for one more hour, casting my lure in a different direction to avoid the car. Nothing. Might as well quit. I reeled in my lure, secure it and carried all my gear to the car.

Sitting in my car, I pulled out my cellphone and punched in to find the number of the police station. With that information, I made the call to the Aurora Police Station.

"Hello, this Sally at the Aurora Police Headquarters. How may I help you?"

"I need to report that there is a car on the bottom of Cherry Creek Basin. It is around 20 feet from the shore line on the east side near the south tip of the basin, If you can send someone within the hour, I'll stay here until they arrive. My cellphone is 719-439-8820. When they arrive, they can call and I'll help then to this direction."

"Thank you for the information. I'll notify the detectives immediately."

***

I waited thirty minutes when I saw the police cars and a large tow truck equipped with a large boom. I was fascinated by the quick procedure of backing to the shore line, and extending the boom over the water. Two officers had slipped on wet suits, mouth pieces, and air tanks.

They jumped in and swam over the car pulling the cables down to it. They soon popped to the surface giving the signal to begin lifting the car. When it was above the water line, the operator retracted the boom, then driving the rig forward enough to lower the car to the concrete. Water was pouring out of the broken windshield and oozing out from around the doors.

"That's a mighty find catch you fellows made so easily, I joking said.

"Yes," said Detective Dorsey, "Not every day do we have this kind of fishing expedition. Delbert, would you go down and look around the bottom of the lake for anything that may have washed out of the car?"

"I can't do that today, Detective. The water is far too cloudy with the muddy water. I'll come back tomorrow when the mud and silt have settled and the water is clear again."

"You are so right. I can see the water is really muddy."

Everyone left. The tow truck hooked onto the drowned car to be taken to the precinct headquarters' yard.

***

The two police officers, Delbert and Andrew, returned the next afternoon. The water was clear enough to see the bottom. They donned their underwater gear and jumped in. They searched in a circle, going wider each time. Delbert found the very tip of a plastic bag sticking out of the mud. When he pulled it out, he saw the license plates. He opened the sack, removed the rocks, then swam to where Andrew was still searching. Delbert pointed up for them to surface. They swam to shore and crawled up the bank.

"These may be the plates for the car. The detectives may have an excellent lead," said Delbert.

"What's that little piece of plastic in the bottom of the bag?" asked Andrew.

Delbert reached in and pulled it out. "Why, it's a VIN tag. Did the person ever jimmy up that strip when trying to remove it. The detectives can read it with the help of a magnifying glass. But the strip can ID the VIN number and owner of the car."

They moved their wet gear, and drove to the police headquarters. They knew they had excellent pieces of evidence for the detectives.

CHAPTER 70
DETECTIVES MICHAEL AND TOM

"**B**oth the Captain and the Commissioner have stated emphatically the we need to arrest the person or persons responsible for the death of the eight men," said Michael.

"We seem to have a ton of forensic reports on the eight. We need to study these and draw some logical conclusions," replied Tom.

"But Tom. We have already done that a few times. We were fortunate to have identified seven who were in the data system. One can't be identified. Why don't we have missing persons' reports? Doesn't the family give a hoot! We can at least get the captain's approval to release the bodies to the seven families," added Michael.

"We had the call of an Edward Blankenship as a person of interest. We know he sold his house far below market values to acquire ready cash. We have an ID on his car and plate numbers. Now we have the report of it being dumped in Cherry Creek Basin. Why would he do that? What is trying to hide? Then the plates and VIN numbers are found in a plastic sack that didn't sink deep enough into the mud. He doesn't know we found his car. He must have done this so our all-points bulletin on his car would be greatly hampered," ventured Tom.

"I agree with all those conclusions. We can now make an educated deduction that he is driving Mrs. Underwood's Dodge with Randy Lawrence's license plates. We need to cancel the bulletin on Blankenship's car and issue a new one with what we logically know," said Michael.

"Yes, I believe that is a valid deduction, Mike. I'll write a new one with the car description and the stolen plate numbers for the National Crime Information Center (NCIC) and have the office make the transmission," replied Tom.

"Blankenship could be long gone from here because of Mrs. Underwood not realizing her car was stolen for three days. Then Lawrence doesn't realize his plates were stolen for three days. I will ask the Commissioner to request the television and radio stations to consider announcing our all-points bulletin as part of their community service. We can add a picture from an auto website of a car like Mrs. Underwood's for the TV stations," said Michael. "I'll ask him now."

"From the profile I composed of all the information we have on Blankenship; I have the intuitive notion that he left Denver for the West coast—Nevada to get lost and a bent for some gambling or California—SanDiego or Los Angeles," said Tom.

"Print out a copy or send the report to my computer so I can read what we know to determine if I can move in on your hunch, as well," requested Michael.

"I" do just that while you see the Commissioner, replied Tom.

***

A week later, no reports of Blankenship's stolen car had been found. "Are we going to have a dead end to this case?" asked Tom.

"Doesn't look good. We can be pleased though with the TV and radio stations running the all-points bulletin plus the NCIC to all law enforcements across the country. We may need to abide our time for someone to see the car. All most like the idea of finding a needle in a hay stack, isn't it," replied Michaael.

CHAPTER 71
ANITA BILLINGS

I was sitting in my office cogitating why I kept running into Howard Jennings as if he knew where I was between my office and showing apartments. His comments and mannerisms have romantic overtones. I don't like it one bit. He makes too many flirtatious remarks, also. What can I do to stop this?

Ah, yes! I'll introduce him to my fiancé. When Howard sees him in his police uniform, that should discourage him from those advances toward me. I picked up my telephone and dialed the police station.

"This is Irene at the Torrance Police Headquarters. How may I direct your call?"

"Hi Irene, this is Anita. Would you connect me to Roger's office?"

"You're in luck, Anita. He is in his office. I'll connect you."

"Hello, Roger."

"Why hello to you my lovely Anita. This a surprise. You rarely call me at work."

"I know, I know that. I'm calling for a special request."

"What would that be, Sweetheart?"

"Would you wear your complete police uniform tonight when you arrive at the apartment? I wish to introduce you to a Howard Jennings that lives here."

"Is there a special reason I don't know to be in my full police attire?""

"Yes, there is. I'll share it with you tonight. Okay? I need to go for my buzzer tells me I need to show some vacancies."

"See you at seven. Buttercup. Good bye till then."

CHAPTER 72
EDWARD BLANKENSHIP AKA HOWARD JENNINGS

t's hot outdoors, but I'll sit here in the shade so I can watch for Anita when she comes out to drive home. She is gorgeous! Just my type of woman. I need to cultivate her friendship. I need to stop with the flirtatious remarks I've been making. I sense she is bothered by them.

Anita came out of the office door. "Hello, Anita. Wow, you look super in that attire. Colors are so well coordinated."

"Well, I do dress differently when going on a date with my fiancée. He should be arriving any moment."

"Oh, I see." *That's not the information I want to hear.*

"There he is now!" Roger drove up alongside of her and got out of the car.

"Howard, this is my finance, Roger. Roger, this is Howard Jennings, who lives here in our apartments."

Roger extended his hand. Howard was forced to do likewise. "So, you are one of the Blue Team of Torrance?"

"That is a correct deduction, Howard. I've been on the force 10 years and one of four detectives."

Howard looked at Roger with a sneer. *He sure as hell is spoiling my plans. Need to find a way to get him out of the picture, somehow.*

Could be tough doing so. "Have you been solving any cases to date? Stolen cars, car jackings, murders."

"Yes we have six cases currently that we are trying to solve. Anita, we need to go. I've made reservations for dinner at the San Franciscan."

"Sounds like a swanky joint," said Howard.

Roger opened the door for Anita. "So long, Howard. See you later." He got in the car and left the parking lot.

See you later. Ha! I'll follow them. Eat at same place near their table. Spoil their love connection.

***

Roger and Anita were seated and ordered a bottle of red wine. After it was poured, Roger held up his glass. "Here's to our pending engagement, my adorable Anita!"

"Thank you, Roger. Here's to you my knight in a police uniform. You are so handsome in it." They tapped glasses.

"Oh, NO!" Here comes Howard. He must have followed us here," said Anita sarcastically.

Howard was seated near Anita and Roger as he requested with the head usher after greasing his hand with a twenty-dollar bill. "Hello, again, you two lovebirds! I came here knowing you knew the best restaurant for dining. I don't."

Roger peered at Howard with a look of disdain. "Howard you can use your cellphone to find the best places to eat. You followed us here on purpose using the excuse you just stated."

"Why heaven's no. I have no cellphone," retorted Howard.

"Then enjoy your meal, Howard. Anita, let's go to another restaurant." Roger threw a twenty-dollar bill on the table to pay for the wine as they stood and left.

I believe I'm getting them flustered. Excellent! Throw a monkey wrench in their love affair. When I get back to the apartment, need to change plates with another California car. Can't be seen with Colorado plates.

CHAPTER 73
ROGER AND ANITA

They entered his car and slowly backed out of the parking space. As Roger drove along the cars to the exit, he saw the brown Dodge with Colorado plates. "That car wasn't there when we parked. It came here after we arrived. Is that Howard's car, perchance?"

"Yes, it is. I see it on the lot by our apartment since he arrived."

Roger pulled out his cellphone and punched in the numbers for his headquarters.

"This is Julia. How may I help you?"

"Julia, this is Roger. Would you find the information on top of my desk that I copied from the NCIC transmission? I'm in my own car now and not my police car so I can't run the plates."

"You wrote down a 2015 brown or dark tan four-door Dodge, License JTL845."

"Thanks, Julia."

"Anita, that's his car alright. Plate numbers are the same. He's wanted by the police in Aurora, Colorado. We need to arrest him and placed in prison until they can get here and take him back to Colorado. Sorry we can't go to dinner now. I'm asking for backup so we can arrest him when he leaves the restaurant and gets into his car."

"That's fine with me. He gives me the creeps! It's good to get rid of him. He was giving me a lot of grief at work and the reason I asked you to wear your full police uniform."

Roger called his precinct headquarters and told Julia of the discovery of the wanted person and the car and asked for backup.

Four police officers who were on patrol in their areas came whipping into the parking lot. The four huddled with Roger. "Park your cars so they can't be seen by Howard. Hide behind the other cars. When he gets into his car, surround it with guns drawn and pointing at him so he understands we mean business. When I direct him to get out of his car, Williard, you cuff him. Bill, read him his rights. Tim, pat him down for any weapons. Chris, train your gun on him at all times," directed Roger.

They crouched behind the other cars. Roger saw Howard walking toward his car. Roger pulled his mic and alerted the four officers. As planned, Howard unlocked his car and got in. All five converged on the Dodge. Roger came up on the passenger's side. He saw Howard reaching for the glove compartment. He slammed the butt of his gun against the window. It shattered. Pointing his gun at Howard, "I would suggest very highly that you do not touch that glove apartment. Get out of the car slowly, reaching for the sky with both arms."

The preplanning was executed without a hitch. Howard was placed in Chris' patrol car and taken to the police headquarters to be booked, and placed in a cell.

Roger and Anita followed the prisoner's car. When Roger arrived at his office, he called the Aurora Police Department and left the detailed information of Howard's capture. "We'll go back to the San Franciscan with the full assurance the Howard will not interfere again."

CHAPTER 74
DETECTIVE MICHAEL

Michael was informed of the capture of Edward Blankenship AKA Howard Jennings the following morning. He called the Torrance Police Headquarters and asked to speak to a Detective Roger Tallman.

"This is Detective Roger Tallman speaking."

"Hello, Detective Roger. This is Detective Michael Dorsey with the Aurora PD. Your message of Blankenship's capture was most pleasing. I presume he did not cause you any trouble."

"No, he was out numbered when five of us surrounded his car that we knew was stolen from the NCIC information."

"He murdered eight men that we know of, then drives a stolen Dodge plus stolen plates of another car, ditched his car in a small lake, and high tailed it to Torrance. We do appreciate your alertness. We were expecting a long dry case before us. Would you be able to get a search warrant approved and comb where he was living, plus the stolen car for additional damaging evidence?"

"Wow, Jennings is one mean hombre. Yes, I'll ask our captain to obtain the warrant and gather any evidence that will help you."

"Our commissioner is getting the approval for me to fly to Los Angeles Airport to take Blankenship off your hands. Today is the fifth, so I will be there on the seventh. I'll call you again for the time the plane lands."

"We'll have transportation waiting for you."

"Thanks. See you on the seventh."

***

Michael arrived at LAX. As planned, Roger met the plane and they were soon enroute to Torrance.

"Michael, we will be able to provide you with a package that contains his gun found in the glove compartment of the car he used. There was a case in his apartment containing syringes and a vial of methamphetamine. There are pictures of dead men. There are some items that you may be able to use. I considered what I could use in solving the case as information you could use."

"Roger, you have done a yeoman's job for us. We really appreciate your solid work. We were hoping against hope that the NCIC report would reach the right place. It was a long shot when his stolen car and plates would be seen. It's a big country with thousands of cars. I said it before. It can be compared to finding a needle in a haystack. But you did it!"

"It certainly helped that he had parked his car close to mine at the restaurant. Had he parked in another area of the lot, I may never have seen the brown car with Colorado plates.

"Well, his bit of carelessness helped you to find him. That's luck or it was meant to be," added Michael.

"We'll impound the stolen car in our yard pending what the owner wants done. Let's get you and your unhappy passenger back to LAX."

***

A subdued man sat beside Miichael on the return flight to Denver. Blankenship's hands were in cuffs attached to a ring fastened to a belt around his waist.

"Are you angry of being caught after all your carefully laid plans disintegrated?' asked Michael.

201

He looked at Michael with a menacing expression that would easily fulfill the saying, if looks could kill, Michael would be dead.

However, Edward's mind was working overtime. *I'll act as though I'm sleeping. When he falls asleep, I'll grab his gun in the holster under his left arm. I'll be in control then. I'll show this dick whose boss.*

What Edward didn't know, is that Michael had given his gun to the airline hostess when boarding who secured it in the galley, to be returned when discharging the plane.

Michael tried to stay awake. A cup of coffee helped, but fatigue settled in and he fell asleep.

Edward saw his chance. He loosened his seat belt. In a desperate move, he stood up partially and fell against Michael, thrashing his hands into Michael's coat for the gun.

Michael woke up with the partial weight of Edward on top of him. Their faces were inches apart staring into each other's eyes.

"Are you satisfied, Mr. Blankenship, to find that I am disarmed? Now would you please sit back in your seat, buckle up, and behave yourself."

The balance of the trip was calm and uneventful. A police car was waiting for Michael's arrival. The prisoner was taken to Aurora Police Headquarters, searched again, booked, given bright orange clothing, placed in a cell, to await arraignment.

Michael drove home satisfied that a murderer was brough to justice—finally.

CHAPTER 75
TOBY AND JOLENE

Toby went to where Jolene was sitting with the cheerleaders in the cafeteria. "Jolene, would you join me for dinner and a movie tonight?" I whispered in her ear.

She fixed her eyes on me seriously and then broke into a charming grin. "Are you asking me for a first date?" she whispered back.

"Yes, you may call it that, Jolene," I said out loud.

"Why, yes. I would enjoy seeing more of you."

"I'll be at your house around 5:30."

"I do wish to introduce you to my mom and dad. Okay?"

"I look forward to meeting them."

***

"Jolene, I can't believe that our high school days are over and graduation is tomorrow. You have come into my life during these past three months since our first date. Our friendship has really grown each day."

"Toby, I have the same da ja Vue, some of my French class vocabulary. One week later, my family will be on vacation to Paris. They are checking out a university for me to attend plus all the sightseeing the city offers. "

"Oh, no, Jolene! I don't want to hear that! I was looking forward to both of us attending college in the area. I would certainly miss you a whole bunch!"

"I would miss you also. I don't know how to thank you for bringing me to the Lord as my personal Savior. My prayers for healing have helped in my mental progress tremendously. I am arriving at the point of being able to forgive those three boys. As a matter of fact, you can tell them that if you make a visit."

"I would be pleased to do that for you. You could go with me and do the forgiveness in person."

"I don't believe I can go that far yet, Toby. I really was surprised at seeing them at graduation. I know you had a big part in their graduating with our class. I really admire you, Toby, in so many ways. You were there for me from the first day of being assaulted. How can I ever thank you for your earnest and valuable help in my healing process. I need to admit, I'm moving from my admiration of you as a dear friend to loving you as the man I have often dreamed about."

"Jolene, my admiration of you as a friend has grown to another wonderful level also. You are indeed a beautiful woman in my eyes. Your acceptance of the Lord has caused you to light up internally and I can see the inner beauty as it unfolds every time I'm in your presence."

"My dearest Toby! Those are the most meaningful, beautiful words I have ever heard about me and I truly cherish them. Kiss me again."

***

"Toby, we have struggled together through four long years at the university. I am so happy I didn't study in Paris. Now what do we do with our lives?"

"Jolene, Sweetheart. With my degree in criminology, I'm going to the police academy and hopefully become a police with the Aurora Police Department."

'Toby, you'll be the best officer on the force! With my degree in French, I plan to finish a Masters Degree in French and apply for a job at the university. I may need to get a doctorate also."

"That is really an ambitious goal. I'll be with you every step of the way. Sweetheart, may I have the pleasure of seeing you and your parents tonight, say 7 p.m.?"

"How formal can we get these days! My dear, Toby, I'll be expecting you."

***

"John and Sally, your beautiful and talented daughter and I have been seeing each other since high school seniors. We studied together through four years of college. I have fallen head over heals in love with her." I reached into my pocket with nervous fingers to find the ring.

"Jolene, will you accept this ring as a token of my love for you to be my wife in the near future?"

"Toby, as I looked at the approving smiles on my parent's faces, yes, I want to be you wife in the near future."

I slipped the ring on her finger followed by a lingering kiss. We could hear her parents softly clapping with words of congratulation."

***

One year later, the wedding was held at the Police Academy. How thrilling to walk between two lines of six police at attention and saluting us. Mike was my best man and Jolene's mother was her maid of honor. The reception followed with family, and many of our high school and university faculty and students.

"You were absolutely stunning, Dear Wife, in that magnificent wedding gown. I love you!"

"And you, my Dear Husband, were also stunning in your full-dress police uniform. I love you!"

I, Toby, was truly in the right place at the right time for my bride is a jewel.

Printed in the United States
by Baker & Taylor Publisher Services